SCIENTIFIC AMERICAN EXPLORES BIG IDEAS

Quantum Concepts

The Editors of *Scientific American*

SCIENTIFIC AMERICAN EDUCATIONAL PUBLISHING

New York

Published in 2023 by Scientific American Educational Publishing
in association with **The Rosen Publishing Group**
2544 Clinton Street, Buffalo NY 14224

Contains material from Scientific American®, a division of Springer Nature America, Inc., reprinted by permission, as well as original material from The Rosen Publishing Group®.

First Edition

Scientific American
Lisa Pallatroni: Project Editor

Rosen Publishing
David Kuchta: Compiling Editor
Michael Moy: Senior Graphic Designer

Cataloging-in-Publication Data
Names: Scientific American.
Title: Quantum concepts / Scientific American.
Description: New York : Scientific American Educational, 2023. | Series: Scientific american explores big ideas | Includes bibliographic information, glossary and index.
Identifiers: ISBN 9781684169399 (pbk) | ISBN 9781684169405 (library bound) | ISBN 9781684169412 (ebook)
Subjects: LCSH: Physics– Juvenile literature | Quantum theory– Juvenile literature
Classification: LCC QC174.14 S35 2023 | DDC 530.12 –dc23

Manufactured in the United States of America
Websites listed were live at the time of publication.

Cover: Jurik Peter/Shutterstock.com

CPSIA Compliance Information: Batch # SACW23.
For Further Information contact Rosen Publishing at 1-800-237-9932.

CONTENTS

Introduction 5

Section 1: The Nature of Reality 6

1.1 100 Years Ago, a Quantum Experiment Explained Why We Don't Fall through Our Chairs 7
By Davide Castelvecchi

1.2 Spooky Quantum Action Passes Test 13
By Ronald Hanson and Krister Shalm

1.3 This Twist on Schrödinger's Cat Paradox Has Major Implications for Quantum Theory 25
By Zeeya Merali

1.4 Quantum Time Twist Offers a Way to Create Schrödinger's Clock 35
By Jonathan O'Callaghan

Section 2: The Quantum Cosmos 37

2.1 Can Quantum Mechanics Save the Cosmic Multiverse? 38
By Yasunori Nomura

2.2 Space: The Final Illusion 48
By Lee Smolin

2.3 What Is Space-Time Really Made Of? 54
By Adam Becker

2.4 Can We Gauge Quantum Time of Flight? 65
By Anil Ananthaswamy

2.5 Could Gravity's Quantum Origins Explain Dark Energy? 73
By Conor Purcell

2.6 Escape from a Black Hole 77
By Steven B. Giddings

2.7 The Cosmological Constant Is Physics' Most Embarrassing Problem 89
By Clara Moskowitz

Section 3: Quantum Technology 99

3.1 Basic Quantum Research Will Transform Science and Industry 100
By Irene Qualters and Antoinette Taylor

3.2 Beyond Quantum Supremacy: The Hunt for Useful Quantum Computers 105
By Michael Brooks

3.3 Race for the Quantum Internet 113
By Lee Billings

3.4 "Hybrid" Quantum Networking Demonstrated for First Time 119
By Dhananjay Khadilkar

3.5 Black Holes, Quantum Entanglement and the No-Go Theorem 123
By Zoë Holmes and Andrew Sornborger

Section 4: Putting Theory to the Test 126

4.1 Unexplained Results Intrigue Physicists at World's Largest Particle Collider 127
By Daniel Garisto

4.2 Elementary Particle's Unexpected Heft Stuns Physicists 131
By Daniel Garisto

4.3 In a First, Physicists Glimpse a Quantum Ghost 136
By Karmela Padavic-Callaghan

4.4 New Views of Quantum Jumps Challenge Core Tenets of Physics 140
By Eleni Petrakou

4.5 The Coolest Physics You've Ever Heard Of 145
By Karmela Padavic-Callaghan

4.6 Will String Theory Finally Be Put to the Experimental Test? 152
By Brendan Z. Foster

Glossary 156
Further Information 157
Citations 158
Index 159

INTRODUCTION

Quantum physics can be as exciting as it can be puzzling. Even after over 100 years of speculation, formulation, and confirmation, it remains one of the cutting edges of science. New insights emerge in the field all the time, challenging our most basic understanding of the world we live in. What is space? What is time? What is matter? What is energy? And as physicist Erwin Schrödinger once famously asked: "What is life?" The articles in this book show how recent developments in quantum physics seek to answer some of those questions.

Section 1, "The Nature of Reality," describes the key principles of quantum theory as they have been developed over the last century and challenged in the last decade. Quantum physics seeks to understand the smallest known particles in our universe–the subatomic world–but in Section 2, "The Quantum Cosmos," we see how it also helps us understand the largest things in our universe, including the universe itself. Section 3, "Quantum Technology," shows how quantum physics is revolutionizing the already revolutionary technologies of the past century: computers and the Internet. And Section 4, "Putting Theory to the Test," examines ways in which there is still so much to learn about the nature of reality, as new insights and experiments challenge us once again to rethink the nature of reality.

Quantum physics is also called theoretical physics for a reason. Nothing at the subatomic level can be seen directly, nor was anyone there to witness the birth of the universe. Answering the most fundamental questions about the world we live in requires as much imagination and creativity as it does scientific rigor. Even Einstein struggled to wrap his head around the concepts he helped develop. But you don't need to be an Einstein to understand quantum physics, as the articles in this book are written not for specialists but for ordinary people with enough curiosity to want to follow this most exciting scientific adventure.

Section 1: The Nature of Reality

1.1 100 Years Ago, a Quantum Experiment Explained Why We Don't Fall through Our Chairs
By Davide Castelvecchi

1.2 Spooky Quantum Action Passes Test
By Ronald Hanson and Krister Shalm

1.3 This Twist on Schrödinger's Cat Paradox Has Major Implications for Quantum Theory
By Zeeya Merali

1.4 Quantum Time Twist Offers a Way to Create Schrödinger's Clock
By Jonathan O'Callaghan

100 Years Ago, a Quantum Experiment Explained Why We Don't Fall through Our Chairs

By Davide Castelvecchi

The moment I meet Horst Schmidt-Böcking outside the Bockenheimer Warte subway stop just north of the downtown area of Frankfurt, Germany, I know I have come to the right place. After my "Hi, thank you for meeting me," his very first words are "I love Otto Stern."

My trip on this pre-pandemic morning in November 2018 is to visit the place that, precisely a century before February 8, 2022, saw one of the most pivotal events for the nascent quantum physics. Without quite realizing what they were seeing, Stern and his fellow physicist and collaborator Walther Gerlach discovered quantum spin: an eternal rotational motion that is intrinsic to elementary particles and that, when measured, only comes in two possible versions—"up" or "down," say, or "left" or "right"—with no other options in between.

Before the Roaring Twenties were over, physicists would reveal spin to be the key to understanding an endless range of everyday phenomena, from the structure of the periodic table to the fact that matter is stable—in other words, the fact that we don't fall through our chair.

But the reason why I have a personal obsession with the Stern-Gerlach experiment—and why I am here in Frankfurt—is that it provided nothing less than a portal for accessing a hidden layer of reality. As physicist Wolfgang Pauli would explain in 1927, spin is quite unlike other physical concepts such as velocities or electric fields. Like those quantities, the spin of an electron is often portrayed as an arrow, but it is an arrow that does not exist in our three dimensions of space. Instead it is found in a 4-D mathematical entity called a Hilbert space.

Schmidt-Böcking–a semi-retired experimentalist at Goethe University Frankfurt and arguably the world's foremost expert on Stern's life and work–is the best guide I could have hoped for. We walk around the block from the station, past the Senckenberg Natural History Museum Frankfurt, to the *Physikalischer Verein*, the local physicists' society, which predates Goethe University Frankfurt's 1914 founding. In this building, in the wee hours of February 8, 1922, Stern and Gerlach shot a beam of silver atoms through a magnetic field and saw that the beam neatly split into two.

Once we are upstairs in the actual room of the experiment, Schmidt-Böcking explains that the whole experimental setup would have fit on a small desk. A vacuum system, made of custom blown-glass parts and sealed with Ramsay grease, enclosed the contraption. I find it hard to picture that in my mind, though, because the room, now windowless, is taken up by some of the nearby museum's collections–specifically, cabinets with tiny specimens of bryozoans, invertebrates that form coral-like colonies.

Stern and Gerlach expected the silver atoms in their beam to act like tiny bar magnets and therefore to react to a magnetic field. As the beam shot horizontally, it squeezed through a narrow gap, with one pole of an electromagnet bracketed above and the other below. It exited the magnet and then hit a screen. When the magnetic field was turned off, the beam would just go straight and deposit a faint dot of silver on the screen, directly in line with the exit path of the beam from the magnet. But when the magnet was switched on, each passing atom experienced a vertical force that depended on the angle of its north-south axis. The force would be strongest upward if north pointed straight up, and it would be strongest downward if north pointed down. But the force could also take any value in between, including zero if the atom's north-south axis was horizontal.

In these circumstances, a magnetic atom that came in at a random angle should have its trajectory deflected by a corresponding random amount, varying along a continuum. As a result, the silver arriving at the screen should have painted a vertical line. At least, that was Stern and Gerlach's "classical" expectation. But that's not what happened.

Unlike classical magnets, the atoms were all deflected by the same amount, either upward or downward, thus splitting the beam into two discrete beams rather than spreading it across a vertical line. "When they did the experiment, they must have been shocked," says Michael Peskin, a theoretical physicist at Stanford University. Like many physicists, Peskin practiced doing the Stern-Gerlach experiment with modern equipment in an undergraduate lab class. "It's really the most amazing thing," he recalls. "You turn on the magnet, and you see these two spots appearing."

Later that day in 2018, I get to see some of the original paraphernalia with my own eyes. Schmidt-Böcking drives me north in Frankfurt to one of the university's campuses, where he keeps the artifacts inside well-padded boxes in his office. The most impressive piece is a high-vacuum pump–a type invented only a few years before the experiment–that removed stray air molecules using a supersonic jet of heated mercury.

It all looks tremendously fragile, and it is: According to witnesses, when the pieces were used, some glass part or other broke virtually every day. Restarting the experiment then required making repairs and pumping the air out again, which took several days. Unlike in modern experiments, the displacement of the beams was tiny–about 0.2 millimeter–and had to be spotted with a microscope.

At the time, Stern was shocked at the outcome. He had conceived the experiment in 1919 as a challenge to what was then the leading hypothesis for the structure of the atom. Formulated by physicist Niels Bohr and others starting in 1913, it pictured electrons like little planets orbiting the atomic nucleus. Only certain orbits were allowed, and jumping between them seemed to provide an accurate explanation for the quanta of light seen in spectroscopic emissions, at least for the simple case of hydrogen. Stern disliked quanta, and together with his friend Max von Laue, he had pledged that "if this nonsense of Bohr should in the end prove to be right, we will quit physics."

To test Bohr's theory, Stern had set about exploring one of its most bizarre predictions, which Bohr himself did not quite believe: that in a magnetic field, atomic orbits can only lie at particular angles. To pursue this experiment, Stern realized that he could look for a magnetic effect of the electron's orbit. He reasoned that the outermost electron of a silver atom, which according to Bohr is orbiting the nucleus in a circle, is an electric charge in motion, and it should therefore produce magnetism.

In Stern and Gerlach's experiment, the physicists detected the splitting of the beam, which they saw as confirmation of Bohr's odd prediction: The atoms got deflected–implying that they were magnetic themselves–and they did so not over a continuum, as in the classical model, but into two separate beams.

It was only after modern quantum mechanics was founded, beginning in 1925, that physicists realized that the silver atom's magnetism is produced not by the orbit of its outermost electron but by that electron's intrinsic spin, which makes it act like a tiny bar magnet. Soon after he heard about of Stern and Gerlach's results, Albert Einstein wrote to the Nobel Foundation to nominate them for a Nobel Prize. But the letter, which Schmidt-Böcking discovered in 2011, was apparently ignored because it nominated other researchers as well, against the foundation's rules. Stern did not quit the field. Eventually he was one of the most Nobel-nominated physicists in history, and he did get his prize in 1943, while World War II was raging.

Stern's prize did not honor his work with Gerlach, however. Instead it was awarded for another tour de force experiment in which Stern and a collaborator measured the magnetism of the proton in 1933–shortly before the Nazi regime drove Stern out of Germany because of his Jewish background. That result was the earliest indication that the proton is not an elementary particle: we now know that it is made of three building blocks called quarks. Gerlach never won a Nobel Prize, perhaps because of his participation in the Nazi regime's attempt to build an atomic bomb.

Today the concept of quantum spin as a 4-D entity is the foundation for all quantum computers. The quantum version of a computer bit, called the qubit, has the same mathematical form as the spin of an electron–whether or not it is in fact encoded in any spinning object. It often is not.

Even so, to this day, physicists continue to argue about how to interpret the experiment. According to now textbook quantum theory, initially, the silver atom's outer electron does not know which way it is spinning. Instead it starts out in a "quantum superposition" of both states–as if its spin were up and down at the same time. The electron does not decide which way it is spinning–and therefore which of the two beams its atom travels in–even after it has skimmed through the magnet. When it has left the magnet and is hurtling toward the screen, the atom splits into two different, coexisting personas, as if it were in two places at the same time: one moves in an upward trajectory, and the other heads downward. The electron only picks one state when its atom arrives at the screen: the atom's position can only be measured when it hits the screen toward the top or bottom–in one of the two spots but not both. Others take what they call a more "realist" approach: the electron knew all along where it was going, and the act of measurement is simply a sorting of the two states that happens at the magnet.

A recent prominent experiment seems to lend added credence to the former interpretation. It suggests that the two personas do coexist when the two spin states are separated. Physicist Ron Folman of Ben-Gurion University of the Negev in Israel and his colleagues re-created the Stern-Gerlach experiment using not individual atoms but a cloud of rubidium atoms. This was cooled to close to absolute zero, which made it act like a single quantum object with its own spin.

The researchers suspended the cloud in a vacuum with a device that can trap atoms and move them around using electric and magnetic fields. Initially, the cloud was in a superposition of spin up and spin down. The team then released it and let it fall by gravity. During its descent, they first applied a magnetic field to separate the atoms into two separate trajectories, according to their spin, just as in the Stern-Gerlach experiment. But unlike in the original experiment, Folman's team then reversed the process and made the two clouds recombine into one. Their measurements showed that the cloud returned into its initial state. The experiment suggests that the separation was reversible and that quantum superposition persisted after being subject to a magnetic field that separated the two spin orientations.

The experiment goes to the heart of what constitutes a measurement in quantum mechanics. Were the spins in the Stern-Gerlach experiment "measured" by the initial sorting done by the magnet? Or did the measurement occur when the atoms hit the screen–or perhaps when the physicists looked at it? Folman's work suggests that wherever a measurement happened, the separation was not at the first stage.

The results are unlikely to quell the philosophical diatribes around the meaning of quantum measurement, says David Kaiser, a physicist and historian of science at the Massachusetts Institute of Technology. But the impact of the Stern-Gerlach experiment remains immense. It led physicists to realize "that there was some internal characteristic of a quantum particle that really doesn't map on to analogies to things like planets and stars," Kaiser says.

About the Author

Davide Castelvecchi is a staff reporter at Nature *who has been obsessed with quantum spin for essentially his entire life.*

Spooky Quantum Action Passes Test

By Ronald Hanson and Krister Shalm

Not all revolutions start big. In the case of quantum mechanics, a quiet one began in 1964, when physicist John Bell published an equation. This equation, in the form of a mathematical inequality, proposed a test to address deep philosophical questions that troubled many of the early founders of quantum mechanics.

The issue was whether particles separated by vast distances could retain a connection so that measurements performed on one would affect the other. According to classical physics, this should be impossible. But under quantum theory, it happens all the time. Through his equation, Bell proposed a way to determine whether the universe could actually be that strange.

Over the past half a century his simple equation has profoundly changed the way we think about quantum theory. Today many of the quantum technologies that physicists are inventing owe their beginnings to Bell's test. Yet it was not until 2015, more than 50 years after Bell proposed his inequality, that scientists were able to verify the predictions of Bell's theorem in the most complete manner possible. These experiments close a quest that has spanned generations and mark the start of a new era in developing quantum technologies.

Hidden Variables

To understand Bell's equation, we must go back to the roots of quantum mechanics. This set of rules describes the behavior of light and matter at the smallest scales. Atoms, electrons, photons and other subatomic particles act differently from things we experience in our everyday lives. One of the major deviations is that these small particles exist in uncertain states. Take an electron's spin, for example. If an electron whose spin is sideways passes through a magnetic field oriented up and down, half the time it will veer upward and half the time it will veer downward, but the outcome is truly random. Compare this to a coin flip. We might think that all coin flips are equally random, but if we knew precisely the mass of the coin, how much force was used to flip it and all the details about the air currents hitting it, we would be able to predict exactly how the coin would land. Electron spin is different, however. Even if we have perfect knowledge about all the properties of the electron and its spin before it passes through the magnetic field, quantum fuzziness prevents us from knowing which way it will go (we can, however, calculate the *probability* of its going up or down). When scientists actually measure a quantum system, though, all these possibilities cease to exist somehow, and a single outcome is decided–the electron ends up having a spin that is oriented either up or down.

When physicists formulated quantum theory in the early 20th century, some of its founding members, such as Albert Einstein and Erwin Schrödinger, felt uncomfortable with the fuzziness of quantum states. Perhaps, they thought, nature is not really fuzzy, and a theory that goes beyond quantum mechanics could exactly predict the behavior of particles. Then it would be possible to foresee the outcome of a measurement of the spin of an electron in the same way it is possible to know exactly how a coin will land if you have enough information.

Schrödinger introduced the idea of entanglement (*Verschränkung* in German) to describe quantum fuzziness spread across two or more particles. According to quantum theory, properties of particles can be entangled such that their joint value is precisely known, but the individual values remain completely uncertain. An analogy would be two dice that, when rolled, would each yield a random result but together always add up to 7. Schrödinger used the idea of entanglement in a famous thought experiment in which the fuzziness of the state of an atom becomes entangled with a cat being dead or alive. Surely any cat is either dead or alive and not in an absurd limbo in between, Schrödinger reasoned, and therefore we should question the notion that atoms can be fuzzy at all.

Einstein, with his collaborators Boris Podolsky and Nathan Rosen (known together as EPR), took the argument a step further by analyzing two entangled electrons that are far apart. Imagine that the spins of the particles are entangled such that when they are measured along the same orientation, opposite values will always result. For instance, if scientists measure one electron spin and find it to be pointing up, the other will point down. Such correlations are certainly surprising when the electrons are far enough apart that it is impossible for them to communicate at the speed of light before their individual spins are measured. How does the second particle know that the first one was up? Einstein famously called this synchronization "spooky action at a distance."

The EPR analysis of this case, published in 1935 in a now classic paper, started from two very reasonable assumptions. First, if scientists can predict a measurement outcome with certainty, there must be some property in nature that corresponds to this outcome. Einstein named these properties "elements of reality." For example, if we know that an electron's spin is up, we can predict with certainty that if it travels through an appropriate magnetic field it will always be deflected upward. In this situation, the electron's spin would be an element of reality because it is well defined and not fuzzy. Second, an event in one place cannot instantaneously affect a faraway event; influences cannot travel faster than the speed of light.

Taking these assumptions, let us analyze two entangled electrons held at distant places by two people, Alice and Bob. Suppose Alice measures her electron spin along the z direction. Because of the perfect anticorrelation, she immediately knows what the outcome will be if Bob measures his electron spin along z as well. According to EPR, the z component of Bob's electron spin would thus be an element of reality. Similarly, if Alice decides to measure the spin along the x direction, she would know with certainty the outcome of a measurement on Bob's electron spin along x. In this case, the x component of Bob's electron spin would be an element of reality. But because Alice and Bob are far apart, Alice's decision to measure along the z direction or the x direction cannot influence what happens at Bob's. Therefore, to account for the perfect anticorrelations predicted by quantum theory, the value of Bob's electron spin must be perfectly predictable along both the z direction and the x direction. This appears to contradict quantum theory, which states, through the so-called Heisenberg uncertainty principle, that the spin can have a well-defined value along a single direction only and must be fuzzy along the others.

This conflict led EPR to conclude that quantum theory is incomplete. They suggested that it might be possible to resolve the contradiction by supplementing the theory with extra variables. In other words, there might be a deeper theory that goes beyond quantum mechanics in which the electrons possess extra properties that describe how they will behave when jointly measured. These extra variables might be hidden from us, but if we had access to them, we could predict exactly what would happen to the electrons. The apparent fuzziness of quantum particles is a result of our ignorance. Physicists call any such successor to quantum mechanics that contains these hidden variables a "local hidden variable theory." The "local" here refers to the hidden signals not being able to travel faster than the speed of light.

Bell's Twist

Einstein did not question the predictions of quantum mechanics itself; rather he believed there was a deeper truth in the form of hidden variables that govern reality. After the 1935 EPR paper, interest in these foundational issues in quantum mechanics died down. The possibility of hidden variables was seen as a philosophical question without any practical value–the predictions of theories with and without hidden variables appeared to be identical. But that changed in 1964, when Bell startlingly showed that in certain circumstances hidden variable theories and quantum mechanics predict different things. This revelation meant it is possible to test experimentally whether local hidden variable theories–and thus Einstein's hoped-for deeper truth of nature–can really exist.

Bell analyzed the EPR thought experiment but with one twist: he let Alice and Bob measure their electron spins along any possible direction. In the traditional experiment, Alice and Bob must measure along the same direction and therefore find that their results are 100 percent correlated–if Alice measures her spin as up, then Bob always measures down. But if Alice and Bob are sometimes measuring along different axes, sometimes their outcomes are not synchronized, and that is where the differences between quantum theory and hidden variable theories come in. Bell showed that for certain sets of directions, the correlations between the outcomes of Alice's and Bob's measurements would be stronger according to quantum theory than according to any local hidden variable theory–a difference known as Bell's inequality. These differences arise because the hidden variables cannot influence one another faster than the speed of light and therefore are limited in how they can coordinate their efforts. In contrast, quantum mechanics allows the two electrons' spins to exist jointly in a single entangled fuzzy state that can stretch over vast distances. Entanglement causes quantum theory to predict correlations that are up to 40 percent stronger.

Bell's theorem completely changed physicists' thinking. It showed a mathematical conflict between Einstein's view and quantum theory and outlined a powerful way for experimentally testing the two. Because Bell's theorem is a mathematical inequality that limits how high correlations can be under any local hidden variable theory, experimental data that exceed these bounds–in other words, that "violate" Bell's inequality–will show that local hidden variable theories cannot describe nature.

Soon after Bell's publication, physicists John Clauser, Michael Horne, Abner Shimony and Richard Holt (known as CHSH) found similar inequalities that were easier to test in experiments. Researchers performed the first trials in the late 1960s, and since then experiments have come closer and closer to the ideal of Bell's proposed setup. The experiments have found correlations that violate Bell's inequality and seemingly cannot be explained by local hidden variable theories. Until 2015, though, all experiments necessarily relied on one or more additional assumptions because of imperfections in the setups. These assumptions provide loopholes that local hidden variable theories could in principle use to pass the test.

In virtually all such experiments in the 20th century, scientists generated entangled photons at a source and sent them to measurement stations (standing in for Alice and Bob). The Alice and Bob stations each measured their respective photon along one of two orientations, noting its polarization–the direction in which the photon's electric field oscillates (polarization can be thought of as the spin of a photon). The scientists then calculated the average correlations between the two stations' outcomes and plugged those into Bell's equation to check whether the results violated the inequality.

Tests With Caveats

The first series of experiments used fixed measurement directions. In these cases, there is ample time for hidden variables (using knowledge of the measurement directions on either side) to influence the outcomes. That is, hidden signals could tell Bob which direction Alice used to measure her photon without traveling faster than light. This so-called locality loophole means that a hidden variable theory could match the quantum correlations. In 1982 French physicist Alain Aspect and his co-workers performed a test where the photons were sent to opposite ends of a large room and their polarization was measured. While these entangled photons were in flight, the polarization angle of the measurement device changed periodically. In the late 1990s Anton Zeilinger, now at the University of Vienna, and his colleagues further improved this strategy by using truly random (as opposed to periodic) polarization-measurement directions. In addition, these measurement directions were determined very shortly before the measurements took place, so hidden signals would have had to travel faster than light to affect this experiment. The locality loophole was firmly closed.

These experiments had one drawback, however: photons are hard to work with. Most of the time the tests got no answer at all, simply because the photons were not created in the first place or were lost along the way. The experimenters were forced to assume that the trials that worked were representative of the full trial set (the "fair sampling assumption"). If this assumption were dropped, the results would not violate Bell's inequality. It is possible that something different was happening in the trials where photons were lost, and if their data were included, the results would not be in conflict with local hidden variable theories. Scientists were able to close this so-called detection loophole in this century by giving up photons and using matter, such as trapped ions, atoms, superconducting circuits and nuclei in diamond atoms, which can all be entangled and measured with high efficiency. The problem is that in these cases the particles were all located extremely close to one another, leaving the locality loophole open. Thus, although these Bell tests were ingenious, they could all, at least in principle, be explained by a local hidden variable theory. A Bell test with all the loopholes closed simultaneously became one of the grandest challenges in quantum science.

Thanks to rapid progress in scientists' ability to control and measure quantum systems, it became possible in 2015, 80 years after the EPR paper and 51 years after Bell's equation, to carry out a Bell test in the ideal setting, often referred to as a loophole-free Bell test. In fact, within a short span of time, four different groups found results that violated Bell's inequality with all loopholes closed–providing ironclad evidence against local hidden variable theories.

Closing the Loopholes

One of us (Hanson) and his collaborators performed the first experiment to close all loopholes at the Delft University of Technology in the Netherlands using a setup that closely resembles the original EPR concept. We entangled the spins of two electrons contained inside a diamond, in a space called a defect center, where a carbon atom should have been but was missing. The two entangled electrons were in different laboratories across campus, and to make sure no communication was possible between them, we used a fast random-number generator to pick the direction of measurement. This measurement was finished and locally recorded on a hard drive before any information from the measurement on the other side could have arrived at light speed. A hidden signal telling one measuring station which direction the other had used would not have had time to travel between the labs, so the locality loophole was firmly closed.

These strict timing conditions required us to separate the two electrons by more than a kilometer, about two orders of magnitude farther apart than the previous world record for entangled matter systems. We achieved this separation by using a technique called entanglement swapping, in which we first entangle each electron with a photon. We then send the photons to meet halfway between the two labs on a semitransparent mirror where we have placed detectors on either side. If we detect the photons on different sides of the mirror, then the spins of the electrons entangled with each photon become entangled themselves. In other words, the entanglement between the electrons and the photons is transferred to the two electrons. This process is prone to failure–photons can be lost between the diamonds and the mirror, just as in the earlier photon-based experiments. But we start a Bell trial only if both photons are detected; thus, we deal with photon loss beforehand. In this way, we close the detection loophole because we do not exclude the findings of any Bell test trials from our final results. Although the photon loss related to the large separation in our case does not limit the quality of the entanglement, it does severely restrict the rate at which we can conduct Bell trials–just a few per hour.

After running the experiment nonstop for several weeks in June 2015, we found Bell's inequality was violated by as much as 20 percent, in full agreement with the predictions of quantum theory. The probability that such results could have arisen in any local hidden variable model–even allowing the devices to have maliciously conspired using all available data–was 0.039. A second experimental run conducted in December 2015 found a similar violation of Bell's inequalities.

In the same year, three other groups performed loophole-free Bell tests. In September physicists at the National Institute of Standards and Technology (NIST) and their colleagues, led by one of us (Shalm), used entangled photons, and in the same month Zeilinger's group did so as well. Not too long after, Harald Weinfurter of Ludwig Maximilian University of Munich and his team used rubidium atoms separated by 400 meters in a scheme similar to that of the Hanson group (the results were published in 2017).

Both the NIST and Vienna teams entangled the polarization state of two photons by using intense lasers to excite a special crystalline material. Very rarely, about one in a billion of the laser photons entering the crystal underwent a transformation and split into a pair of daughter photons whose polarization states were entangled. With powerful enough lasers, it was possible to generate tens of thousands of entangled photon pairs per second. We then sent these photons to distant stations (separated by 184 meters in the NIST experiment and 60 meters in the Vienna experiment) where we measured the polarization states. While the photons were in flight toward the measurement stations, our system decided in which direction to measure their polarization such that it would be impossible for any hidden variables to influence the results. The locality loophole was therefore closed. The most challenging aspect of using photons is preventing them from being lost because we must detect more than two thirds of the photons we create in our setup to avoid the detection loophole. Most conventional single-photon detectors operate at around 60 percent efficiency–a nonstarter for this test. But at NIST we developed special single-photon detectors, made of cold superconducting materials, capable of observing more than 90 percent of the photons that reach it. Thus, we closed the detection loophole as well.

Repeating these polarization measurements on many different entangled photon pairs more than 100,000 times per second, we were able to quickly accumulate statistics on the correlations between the photon polarization states. The correlations observed in both experiments were much stronger than those predicted by hidden variable theories. In fact, the probability that the NIST results could have arisen by chance is on the order of one in a billion (even less likely than winning the Powerball lottery), and the chances are even smaller for the Vienna experiment. Today our NIST group regularly uses an improved version of our setup to violate Bell's inequalities to a similar degree in less than a minute, and future improvements will speed this up by two orders of magnitude.

Harnessing Entanglement

These experiments force us to conclude that any local hidden variable model, such as those Einstein advocated, is incompatible with nature. The correlations between particles we have observed defy our intuition, showing that spooky action does indeed take place.

Our results also hint at the remarkable power contained in entanglement that we may be able to put to use. A near-term application where loophole-free Bell tests can be useful is in generating randomness. Random numbers are a critical resource in many cryptographic and security techniques. If you can predict the next number a random-number generator will produce, you can hack many financial and communications systems. A good source of randomness that cannot be predicted is therefore of vital importance. Two of the most common ways to generate randomness are through mathematical algorithms and by using physical processes. With mathematical algorithms, if you know the conditions used as a "seed," you can often predict the output perfectly. With physical processes, a detailed understanding of the underlying physics of the system is required. Miss even a single detail, and a hacker can exploit or control the randomness. The history of cryptography is littered with examples of both types of random-number generators being broken.

Quantum mechanics has handed us a gift, though. It is possible to "extract" the randomness inherent in quantum processes to produce true randomness. The correlations measured in a loophole-free Bell test can be distilled into a certifiably random string. Remarkably, it is possible to hand part of the experimental apparatus (the generation of the entangled particles) to a potential hacker to control. Even in this extreme case, it is possible to produce numbers that are as random as nature allows. In early 2018 our team at NIST was able to use our loophole-free Bell setup to extract 1,024 truly random bits from 10 minutes of experimental data. These bits were certified as random to better than a part in one trillion. In contrast, it would take a conventional random-number generator several hundred thousand years to acquire enough data to directly measure the quality of their randomness to this level. We are working now to incorporate our random-number generator into a public randomness beacon. This tool could act as a time-stamped source of random numbers that is broadcast over the Internet at fixed intervals and can be used in security applications by anyone who needs it.

On a more general level, the techniques developed in loophole-free Bell experiments may enable fundamentally new types of communications networks. Such networks, often referred to as a quantum Internet, can perform tasks that are out of reach of classical information networks. A quantum Internet could enable secure communication, clock synchronization, quantum-sensor networks, and access to remote quantum computers in the cloud. Another goal is "device-independent cryptography," in which (in close analogy to the randomness beacon) users can validate the secrecy of a shared key through a violation of Bell's inequalities.

The backbone of a future quantum Internet will be formed by entanglement links precisely like the setups used to test Bell's inequalities with diamond defect centers, trapped atoms and photons. In 2017 our team at Delft demonstrated a method to boost the quality of remote entangled spins, and in 2018 we improved the entangling rates by three orders of magnitude. Based on this progress, researchers began working toward a first rudimentary version of a quantum Internet.

Eight decades ago when quantum theory was being written, skeptics chafed at its apparent contradiction of the centuries of physical intuition that had been developed; now four experiments have dealt the final blow to that intuition. At the same time, these results have opened the door to exploit nature in ways that Einstein and Bell could not have foreseen. The quiet revolution that John Bell kicked off is now in full swing.

About the Authors

Ronald Hanson is a physicist at the Delft University of Technology and scientific director of its QuTech research center, a collaboration with the Netherlands Organization for Applied Scientific Research (TNO), focused on quantum computing and quantum Internet technology.

Krister Shalm is a physicist at the National Institute of Standards and Technology and the University of Colorado Boulder, where he develops tools to test foundational issues in quantum mechanics.

This Twist on Schrödinger's Cat Paradox Has Major Implications for Quantum Theory

By Zeeya Merali

What does it feel like to be both alive and dead?

That question irked and inspired Hungarian-American physicist Eugene Wigner in the 1960s. He was frustrated by the paradoxes arising from the vagaries of quantum mechanics—the theory governing the microscopic realm that suggests, among many other counter-intuitive things, that until a quantum system is observed, it does not necessarily have definite properties. Take his fellow physicist Erwin Schrödinger's famous thought experiment in which a cat is trapped in a box with poison that will be released if a radioactive atom decays. Radioactivity is a quantum process, so before the box is opened, the story goes, the atom has both decayed and not decayed, leaving the unfortunate cat in limbo—a so-called superposition between life and death. But does the cat experience being in superposition?

Wigner sharpened the paradox by imagining a (human) friend of his shut in a lab, measuring a quantum system. He argued it was absurd to say his friend exists in a superposition of having seen and not seen a decay unless and until Wigner opens the lab door. "The 'Wigner's friend' thought experiment shows that things can become very weird if the observer is also observed," says Nora Tischler, a quantum physicist at Griffith University in Brisbane, Australia.

Now Tischler and her colleagues have carried out a version of the Wigner's friend test. By combining the classic thought experiment with another quantum head-scratcher called entanglement—a phenomenon that links particles across vast distances—they have also derived a new theorem, which they claim puts the strongest constraints yet on the fundamental nature of reality. Their study, which appeared in *Nature Physics*, has implications for the role that consciousness might play in quantum physics—and even whether quantum theory must be replaced.

The new work is an "important step forward in the field of experimental metaphysics," says quantum physicist Aephraim Steinberg of the University of Toronto, who was not involved in the study. "It's the beginning of what I expect will be a huge program of research."

A Matter of Taste

Until quantum physics came along in the 1920s, physicists expected their theories to be deterministic, generating predictions for the outcome of experiments with certainty. But quantum theory appears to be inherently probabilistic. The textbook version—sometimes called the Copenhagen interpretation—says that until a system's properties are measured, they can encompass myriad values. This superposition only collapses into a single state when the system is observed, and physicists can never precisely predict what that state will be. Wigner held the then popular view that consciousness somehow triggers a superposition to collapse. Thus, his hypothetical friend would discern a definite outcome when she or he made a measurement—and Wigner would never see her or him in superposition.

This view has since fallen out of favor. "People in the foundations of quantum mechanics rapidly dismiss Wigner's view as spooky and ill-defined because it makes observers special," says David Chalmers, a philosopher and cognitive scientist at New York University. Today most physicists concur that inanimate objects can knock quantum systems out of superposition through a process known as decoherence. Certainly, researchers attempting to manipulate complex quantum superpositions in the lab can find their hard work destroyed by speedy air particles colliding with their systems. So they carry out their tests at ultracold temperatures and try to isolate their apparatuses from vibrations.

Several competing quantum interpretations have sprung up over the decades that employ less mystical mechanisms, such as decoherence, to explain how superpositions break down without invoking consciousness. Other interpretations hold the even more radical position that there is no collapse at all. Each has its own weird and wonderful take on Wigner's test. The most exotic is the "many worlds" view, which says that whenever you make a quantum measurement, reality fractures, creating parallel universes to accommodate every possible outcome. Thus, Wigner's friend would split into two copies and, "with good enough supertechnology," he could indeed measure that person to be in superposition from outside the lab, says quantum physicist and many-worlds fan Lev Vaidman of Tel Aviv University.

The alternative "Bohmian" theory (named for physicist David Bohm) says that at the fundamental level, quantum systems do have definite properties; we just do not know enough about those systems to precisely predict their behavior. In that case, the friend has a single experience, but Wigner may still measure that individual to be in a superposition because of his own ignorance. In contrast, a relative newcomer on the block called the QBism interpretation embraces the probabilistic element of quantum theory wholeheartedly (QBism, pronounced "cubism," is actually short for quantum Bayesianism, a reference to 18th-century mathematician Thomas Bayes's work on probability.) QBists argue that a person can only use quantum mechanics to calculate how to calibrate his or her beliefs about what he or she will measure in an experiment. "Measurement outcomes must be regarded as personal to the agent who makes the measurement," says Ruediger Schack of Royal Holloway, University of London, who is one of QBism's founders. According to QBism's tenets, quantum theory cannot tell you anything about the underlying state of reality, nor can Wigner use it to speculate on his friend's experiences.

Another intriguing interpretation, called retrocausality, allows events in the future to influence the past. "In a retrocausal account, Wigner's friend absolutely does experience something," says Ken Wharton, a physicist at San Jose State University, who is an advocate for this time-twisting view. But that "something" the friend experiences at the point of measurement can depend upon Wigner's choice of how to observe that person later.

The trouble is that each interpretation is equally good–or bad–at predicting the outcome of quantum tests, so choosing between them comes down to taste. "No one knows what the solution is," Steinberg says. "We don't even know if the list of potential solutions we have is exhaustive."

Other models, called collapse theories, do make testable predictions. These models tack on a mechanism that forces a quantum system to collapse when it gets too big–explaining why cats, people and other macroscopic objects cannot be in superposition. Experiments are underway to hunt for signatures of such collapses, but as yet they have not found anything. Quantum physicists are also placing ever larger objects into superposition: last year a team in Vienna reported doing so with a 2,000-atom molecule. Most quantum interpretations say there is no reason why these efforts to supersize superpositions should not continue upward forever, presuming researchers can devise the right experiments in pristine lab conditions so that decoherence can be avoided. Collapse theories, however, posit that a limit will one day be reached, regardless of how carefully experiments are prepared. "If you try and manipulate a classical observer–a human, say–and treat it as a quantum system, it would immediately collapse," says Angelo Bassi, a quantum physicist and proponent of collapse theories at the University of Trieste in Italy.

A Way to Watch Wigner's Friend

Tischler and her colleagues believed that analyzing and performing a Wigner's friend experiment could shed light on the limits of quantum theory. They were inspired by a new wave of theoretical and experimental papers that have investigated the role of the observer in quantum theory by bringing entanglement into Wigner's classic setup. Say you take two particles of light, or photons, that are polarized so that they can vibrate horizontally or vertically. The photons can also be placed in a superposition of vibrating both horizontally and vertically at the same time, just as Schrödinger's paradoxical cat can be both alive and dead before it is observed.

Such pairs of photons can be prepared together–entangled–so that their polarizations are always found to be in the opposite direction when observed. That may not seem strange–unless you remember that these properties are not fixed until they are measured. Even if one photon is given to a physicist called Alice in Australia, while the other is transported to her colleague Bob in a lab in Vienna, entanglement ensures that as soon as Alice observes her photon and, for instance, finds its polarization to be horizontal, the polarization of Bob's photon instantly syncs to vibrating vertically. Because the two photons appear to communicate faster than the speed of light–something prohibited by his theories of relativity–this phenomenon deeply troubled Albert Einstein, who dubbed it "spooky action at a distance."

These concerns remained theoretical until the 1960s, when physicist John Bell devised a way to test if reality is truly spooky–or if there could be a more mundane explanation behind the correlations between entangled partners. Bell imagined a commonsense theory that was local–that is, one in which influences could not travel between particles instantly. It was also deterministic rather than inherently probabilistic, so experimental results could, in principle, be predicted with certainty, if only physicists understood more about the system's hidden properties. And it was realistic, which, to a quantum theorist, means that systems would have these definite properties even if nobody looked at them. Then Bell calculated the maximum level of correlations between a series of entangled particles that such a local, deterministic and realistic theory could support. If that threshold was violated in an experiment, then one of the assumptions behind the theory must be false.

Such "Bell tests" have since been carried out, with a series of watertight versions performed in 2015, and they have confirmed reality's spookiness. "Quantum foundations is a field that was really started experimentally by Bell's [theorem]–now over 50 years old. And we've spent a lot of time re-implementing those experiments and discussing what they mean," Steinberg says. "It's very rare that people are able to come up with a new test that moves beyond Bell."

The Brisbane team's aim was to derive and test a new theorem that would do just that, providing even stricter constraints—"local friendliness" bounds—on the nature of reality. Like Bell's theory, the researchers' imaginary one is local. They also explicitly ban "superdeterminism"—that is, they insist that experimenters are free to choose what to measure without being influenced by events in the future or the distant past. (Bell implicitly assumed that experimenters can make free choices, too.) Finally, the team prescribes that when an observer makes a measurement, the outcome is a real, single event in the world—it is not relative to anyone or anything.

Testing local friendliness requires a cunning setup involving two "superobservers," Alice and Bob (who play the role of Wigner), watching their friends Charlie and Debbie. Alice and Bob each have their own interferometer—an apparatus used to manipulate beams of photons. Before being measured, the photons' polarizations are in a superposition of being both horizontal and vertical. Pairs of entangled photons are prepared such that if the polarization of one is measured to be horizontal, the polarization of its partner should immediately flip to be vertical. One photon from each entangled pair is sent into Alice's interferometer, and its partner is sent to Bob's. Charlie and Debbie are not actually human friends in this test. Rather, they are beam displacers at the front of each interferometer. When Alice's photon hits the displacer, its polarization is effectively measured, and it swerves either left or right, depending on the direction of the polarization it snaps into. This action plays the role of Alice's friend Charlie "measuring" the polarization. (Debbie similarly resides in Bob's interferometer.)

Alice then has to make a choice: She can measure the photon's new deviated path immediately, which would be the equivalent of opening the lab door and asking Charlie what he saw. Or she can allow the photon to continue on its journey, passing through a second beam displacer that recombines the left and right paths—the equivalent of keeping the lab door closed. Alice can then directly measure her photon's polarization as it exits the interferometer. Throughout the experiment, Alice and Bob independently choose which measurement choices to make and then compare notes to calculate the correlations seen across a series of entangled pairs.

Tischler and her colleagues carried out 90,000 runs of the experiment. As expected, the correlations violated Bell's original bounds–and crucially, they also violated the new local-friendliness threshold. The team could also modify the setup to tune down the degree of entanglement between the photons by sending one of the pair on a detour before it entered its interferometer, gently perturbing the perfect harmony between the partners. When the researchers ran the experiment with this slightly lower level of entanglement, they found a point where the correlations still violated Bell's bound but not local friendliness. This result proved that the two sets of bounds are not equivalent and that the new local-friendliness constraints are stronger, Tischler says. "If you violate them, you learn more about reality," she adds. Namely, if your theory says that "friends" can be treated as quantum systems, then you must either give up locality, accept that measurements do not have a single result that observers must agree on or allow superdeterminism. Each of these options has profound–and, to some physicists, distinctly distasteful–implications.

Reconsidering Reality

"The paper is an important philosophical study," says Michele Reilly, co-founder of Turing, a quantum-computing company based in New York City, who was not involved in the work. She notes that physicists studying quantum foundations have often struggled to come up with a feasible test to back up their big ideas. "I am thrilled to see an experiment behind philosophical studies," Reilly says. Steinberg calls the experiment "extremely elegant" and praises the team for tackling the mystery of the observer's role in measurement head-on.

Although it is no surprise that quantum mechanics forces us to give up a commonsense assumption–physicists knew that from

Bell—"the advance here is that we are a narrowing in on which of those assumptions it is," says Wharton, who was also not part of the study. Still, he notes, proponents of most quantum interpretations will not lose any sleep. Fans of retrocausality, such as himself, have already made peace with superdeterminism: in their view, it is not shocking that future measurements affect past results. Meanwhile QBists and many-worlds adherents long ago threw out the requirement that quantum mechanics prescribes a single outcome that every observer must agree on.

And both Bohmian mechanics and spontaneous collapse models already happily ditched locality in response to Bell. Furthermore, collapse models say that a real macroscopic friend cannot be manipulated as a quantum system in the first place.

Vaidman, who was also not involved in the new work, is less enthused by it, however, and criticizes the identification of Wigner's friend with a photon. The methods used in the paper "are ridiculous; the friend has to be macroscopic," he says. Philosopher of physics Tim Maudlin of New York University, who was not part of the study, agrees. "Nobody thinks a photon is an observer, unless you are a panpsychic," he says. Because no physicist questions whether a photon can be put into superposition, Maudlin feels the experiment lacks bite. "It rules something out—just something that nobody ever proposed," he says.

Tischler accepts the criticism. "We don't want to overclaim what we have done," she says. The key for future experiments will be scaling up the size of the "friend," adds team member Howard Wiseman, a physicist at Griffith University. The most dramatic result, he says, would involve using an artificial intelligence, embodied on a quantum computer, as the friend. Some philosophers have mused that such a machine could have humanlike experiences, a position known as the strong AI hypothesis, Wiseman notes, though nobody yet knows whether that idea will turn out to be true. But if the hypothesis holds, this quantum-based artificial general intelligence (AGI) would be microscopic. So from the point of view of spontaneous collapse models, it would not trigger collapse because of its size. If such a test was run, and the local-friendliness bound was not violated, that result would imply that an AGI's consciousness cannot be put into superposition. In turn, that conclusion would suggest that Wigner was right that consciousness causes collapse. "I don't think I will live to see an experiment like this," Wiseman says. "But that would be revolutionary."

Reilly, however, warns that physicists hoping that future AGI will help them home in on the fundamental description of reality are putting the cart before the horse. "It's not inconceivable to me that quantum computers will be the paradigm shift to get to us into AGI," she says. "Ultimately, we need a theory of everything in order to build an AGI on a quantum computer, period, full stop."

That requirement may rule out more grandiose plans. But the team also suggests more modest intermediate tests involving machine-learning systems as friends, which appeals to Steinberg. That approach is "interesting and provocative," he says. "It's becoming conceivable that larger- and larger-scale computational devices could, in fact, be measured in a quantum way."

Renato Renner, a quantum physicist at the Swiss Federal Institute of Technology Zurich (ETH Zurich), makes an even stronger claim: regardless of whether future experiments can be carried out, he says, the new theorem tells us that quantum mechanics needs to be replaced. In 2018 Renner and his colleague Daniela Frauchiger, then at ETH Zurich, published a thought experiment based on Wigner's friend and used it to derive a new paradox. Their setup differs from that of the Brisbane team but also involves four observers whose measurements can become entangled. Renner and Frauchiger calculated that if the observers apply quantum laws to one another, they can end up inferring different results in the same experiment.

"The new paper is another confirmation that we have a problem with current quantum theory," says Renner, who was not involved in the work. He argues that none of today's quantum interpretations can worm their way out of the so-called Frauchiger-Renner paradox without proponents admitting they do not care whether quantum theory gives consistent results. QBists offer the most palatable means of escape, because from the outset, they say that quantum theory cannot be used to infer what other observers will measure, Renner says. "It still worries me, though: If everything is just personal to me, how can I say anything relevant to you?" he adds. Renner is now working on a new theory that provides a set of mathematical rules that would allow one observer to work out what another should see in a quantum experiment.

Still, those who strongly believe their favorite interpretation is right see little value in Tischler's study. "If you think quantum mechanics is unhealthy, and it needs replacing, then this is useful because it tells you new constraints," Vaidman says. "But I don't agree that this is the case–many worlds explains everything."

For now, physicists will have to continue to agree to disagree about which interpretation is best or if an entirely new theory is needed. "That's where we left off in the early 20th century–we're genuinely confused about this," Reilly says. "But these studies are exactly the right thing to do to think through it."

About the Author

Zeeya Merali is a freelance writer based in London and author of A Big Bang in a Little Room.

Quantum Time Twist Offers a Way to Create Schrödinger's Clock

By Jonathan O'Callaghan

Albert Einstein's twin paradox is one of the most famous thought experiments in physics. It postulates that if you send one of two twins on a return trip to a star at near light speed, they will be younger than their identical sibling when they return home. The age difference is a consequence of something called time dilation, which is described by Einstein's special theory of relativity: the faster you travel, the slower time appears to pass.

But what if we introduce quantum theory into the problem? Physicists Alexander Smith of Saint Anselm College and Dartmouth College and Mehdi Ahmadi of Santa Clara University tackle this idea in a study published in the journal *Nature Communications*. The scientists imagine measuring a quantum atomic clock experiencing two different times while it is placed in superposition–a quirk of quantum mechanics in which something appears to exist in two places at once. "We know from Einstein's special theory of relativity that when a clock moves relative to another clock, the time shown on it slows down," Smith says. "But quantum mechanics allows you to start thinking about what happens if this clock were to move in a superposition of two different speeds."

Superposition is a strange aspect of quantum physics where an object can initially be in multiple locations simultaneously, yet when it is observed, only one of those states becomes true. Particles can be placed in superposition in certain experiments, such as those using a beam splitter to divide photons of light, to show the phenomenon in action. Both of the particles in superposition appear to share information until they are observed, making the phenomenon useful for applications such as encryption and quantum communications.

Some atoms, meanwhile, can act as atomic clocks, with their rate of decay noting the passage of time. In their paper, Smith and

Ahmadi describe how an atomic clock placed in superposition could experience time dilation, just like Einstein's twins experiment, if one of the superposition states is moved at several meters per second while the other remains stationary. Instead of the atom simply being in two states at once–as described in the Schrödinger's cat experiment–the states would actually age differently. "It's kind of like 'Schrödinger's clock,'" Smith says.

Vlatko Vedral, a physicist at the University of Oxford, who was not involved in the study, says the idea allows for a rare opportunity to merge quantum mechanics with relativity–two areas of physics that infamously do not mix well. "You can actually combine the superposition principle in quantum mechanics with this notion of time dilation in relativity," he says. "It's exactly Einstein's twins but now applied to the same system. That's the twist. The final state is really amazing, because the atom is back in the same position where you started, but internally, it feels two different times. It's in a superposition of being older and younger at the same time."

Though the effect is far too small to be noticeable to humans, this idea of quantum time dilation could have repercussions for high-precision quantum clocks. And crucially, the new study suggests it might be possible to measure the effect experimentally. "I'm hoping this paper really prompts people to try to do this in the lab," Vedral says. And Smith suggests an experimental proposal could be drafted in the near future, perhaps using spectroscopy to split light, to look for this signature of quantum time dilation. "We might be able to see this in the next five to 10 years," he says. "I don't think it's science fiction by any means."

About the Author

Jonathan O'Callaghan is a freelance journalist covering commercial spaceflight, space exploration, and astrophysics.

Section 2: The Quantum Cosmos

2.1 Can Quantum Mechanics Save the Cosmic Multiverse?
By Yasunori Nomura

2.2 Space: The Final Illusion
By Lee Smolin

2.3 What Is Space-time Really Made Of?
By Adam Becker

2.4 Can We Gauge Quantum Time of Flight?
By Anil Ananthaswamy

2.5 Could Gravity's Quantum Origins Explain Dark Energy?
By Conor Purcell

2.6 Escape from a Black Hole
By Steven B. Giddings

2.7 The Cosmological Constant Is Physics' Most Embarrassing Problem
By Clara Moskowitz

Can Quantum Mechanics Save the Cosmic Multiverse?

By Yasunori Nomura

Many cosmologists now accept the extraordinary idea that what seems to be the entire universe may actually be only a tiny part of a much larger structure called the multiverse. In this picture, multiple universes exist, and the rules we once assumed were basic laws of nature take different forms in each; for example, the types and properties of elementary particles may differ from one universe to another. The multiverse idea emerges from a theory that suggests the very early cosmos expanded exponentially. During this period of "inflation," some regions would have halted their rapid expansion sooner than others, forming what are called bubble universes, much like bubbles in boiling water. Our universe would be just one of these bubbles, and beyond it would lie infinitely more.

The idea that our entire universe is only a part of a much larger structure is, by itself, not as outlandish as it sounds. Throughout history scientists have learned many times over that the visible world is far from all there is. Yet the multiverse notion, with its unlimited number of bubble universes, does present a major theoretical problem: it seems to erase the ability of the theory to make predictions—a central requirement of any useful theory. In the words of Alan Guth of the Massachusetts Institute of Technology, one of the creators of inflation theory, "in an eternally inflating universe, anything that can happen will happen; in fact, it will happen an infinite number of times."

In a single universe where events occur a finite number of times, scientists can calculate the relative probability of one event occurring versus another by comparing the number of times these events happen. Yet in a multiverse where everything happens an infinite number of times, such counting is not possible, and nothing is more likely to occur than anything else. One can make any prediction one wants, and it is bound to come true in some universe, but that fact tells you nothing about what will go on in our specific world.

This apparent loss of predictive power has long troubled physicists. Some researchers, including me, have now realized that quantum theory–which, in contrast to the multiverse notion, is concerned with the very smallest particles in existence–may, ironically, point the way to a solution. Specifically, the cosmological picture of the eternally inflating multiverse may be mathematically equivalent to the "many worlds" interpretation of quantum mechanics, which attempts to explain how particles can seem to be in many places at once. As we will see, such a connection between the theories does not just solve the prediction problem; it may also reveal surprising truths about space and time.

Quantum Many Worlds

I came to the idea of a correspondence between the two theories after I revisited the tenets of the many-worlds interpretation of quantum mechanics. This concept arose to make sense of some of the stranger aspects of quantum physics. In the quantum world–a nonintuitive place–cause and effect work differently than they do in the macro world, and the outcome of any process is always probabilistic. Whereas in our macroscopic experience, we can predict where a ball will land when it is thrown based on its starting point, speed and other factors, if that ball were a quantum particle, we could only ever say it has a certain chance of ending up here and another chance of ending up there. This probabilistic nature cannot be avoided by knowing more about the ball, the air currents or such details; it is an intrinsic property of the quantum realm. The same exact ball thrown under the same exact conditions will sometimes land at point A and other times at point B. This conclusion may seem strange, but the laws of quantum mechanics have been confirmed by innumerable experiments and truly describe how nature works at the scale of subatomic particles and forces.

In the quantum world, we say that after the ball is thrown, but before we look for its landing spot, it is in a so-called superposition state of outcomes A and B–that is, it is neither at point A nor at point B but located in a probabilistic haze of *both* points A and B (and many other locations as well). Once we look, however, and find the ball in a certain place–say, point A–then anyone else who examines the ball will also confirm that it sits at A. In other words, before any quantum system is measured, its outcome is uncertain, but afterward all subsequent measurements will find the same result as the first.

In the conventional understanding of quantum mechanics, called the Copenhagen interpretation, scientists explain this shift by saying that the first measurement changed the state of the system from a superposition state to the state A. But although the Copenhagen interpretation does predict the outcomes of laboratory experiments, it leads to serious difficulties at the conceptual level. What does the "measurement" really mean, and why does it change the state of the system from a superposition of possibilities to a single certainty? Does the change of state occur when a dog or even a fly observes the system? What about when a molecule in the air interacts with the system, which we expect to be occurring all the time yet which we do not usually treat as a measurement that can interfere with the outcome? Or is there some special physical significance in a human consciously learning the state of the system?

In 1957 Hugh Everett, then a graduate student at Princeton University, developed the many-worlds interpretation of quantum mechanics that beautifully addresses this issue–although at the time many received it with ridicule, and the idea is still less favored than the Copenhagen interpretation. Everett's key insight was that the state of a quantum system reflects the state of the *whole* universe around it, so that we must include the observer in a complete description of the measurement. In other words, we cannot consider the ball, the wind and the hand that throws it in isolation–we must also include in the fundamental description the person who comes along to inspect its landing spot, as well as everything else in the cosmos at that time. In this picture, the quantum state after the measurement is still a superposition–a superposition of not just two landing spots but two entire worlds! In the first world, the observer finds that the state of the system has changed to A, and therefore any observer in this particular world will obtain result A in all subsequent measurements. But when the measurement was made, another universe split off from the first in which the observer finds, and keeps finding, that the ball landed at point B. This feature explains why the observer–let us say it is a man–thinks that his measurement changes the state of the system; what actually happens is that when he makes a measurement (interacts with the system), he himself divides into two different people who live in two different parallel worlds corresponding to two separate outcomes, A and B.

According to this picture, humans making measurements have no special significance. The state of the entire world continuously branches into many possible parallel worlds that coexist as a superposition. A human observer, being a part of nature, cannot escape from this cycle–the observer keeps splitting into many observers living in many possible parallel worlds, and all are equally "real." An obvious but important implication of this picture is that everything in nature obeys the laws of quantum mechanics, whether small or large.

What does this interpretation of quantum mechanics have to do with the multiverse discussed earlier, which seems to exist in a continuous real space rather than as parallel realities? In 2011 I argued that the eternally inflating multiverse and quantum-mechanical many worlds à la Everett are the same concept in a specific sense. In this understanding, the infinitely large space associated with eternal inflation is a kind of "illusion"–the many bubble universes of inflation do not all exist in a single real space but represent the possible different branches on the probabilistic tree. Around the same time that I made this proposal, Raphael Bousso of the University of California, Berkeley, and Leonard Susskind of Stanford University put forth a similar idea. If true, the many-worlds interpretation of the multiverse would mean that the laws of quantum mechanics do not operate solely in the microscopic realm—they also play a crucial role in determining the global structure of the multiverse even at the largest distance scales.

Black Hole Quandary

To better explain how the many-worlds interpretation of quantum mechanics could describe the inflationary multiverse, I must digress briefly to talk about black holes. Black holes are extreme warps in space-time whose powerful gravity prevents objects that fall into them from escaping. As such, they provide an ideal testing ground for physics involving strong quantum and gravitational effects. A particular thought experiment about these entities reveals where the traditional way of thinking about the multiverse goes off track, thereby making prediction impossible.

Suppose we drop a book into a black hole and observe from the outside what happens. Whereas the book itself can never escape the black hole, theory predicts that the information in the book will not be lost. After the book has been shredded by the black hole's gravity and after the black hole itself has gradually evaporated by emitting faint radiation (a phenomenon known as Hawking radiation, discovered by physicist Stephen Hawking of the University of Cambridge), outside observers can reconstruct all the information contained in the initial book by closely examining the radiation released. Even before the black hole has completely evaporated, the book's information starts to slowly leak out via each piece of Hawking radiation.

Yet a puzzling thing occurs if we think about the same situation from the viewpoint of someone who is falling into the black hole along with the book. In this case, the book seems to simply pass through the boundary of the black hole and stay inside. Thus, to this inside observer, the information in the book is also contained within the black hole forever. On the other hand, we have just argued that from a distant observer's point of view, the information will be *outside*. Which is correct? You might think that the information is simply duplicated: one copy inside and the other outside. Such a solution, however, is impossible. In quantum mechanics, the so-called no-cloning theorem prohibits faithful, full copying of information. Therefore, it seems that the two pictures seen by the two observers cannot both be true.

Physicists Gerard 't Hooft of Utrecht University in the Netherlands, Susskind and their collaborators have proposed the following solution: the two pictures can both be valid but not at the same time. If you are a distant observer, then the information is outside. You need not describe the interior of the black hole, because you can never access it even in principle; in fact, to avoid cloning information, you must think of the interior space-time as nonexistent. In contrast, if you are an observer falling into the hole, then the interior is all you have, and it contains the book and its information. This view, however, is possible only at the cost of ignoring the Hawking radiation being emitted from the black hole–but such a conceit is allowed because you yourself have crossed the black hole boundary and accordingly are trapped inside, cut off from the radiation emitted from the boundary. There is no inconsistency in either of these two viewpoints; only if you artificially "patch" the two–which you can never physically do, given that you cannot be both a distant and a falling observer at the same time–does the apparent inconsistency of information cloning occur.

Cosmological Horizons

This black hole conundrum may seem unrelated to the issue of how the many-worlds notion of quantum mechanics and the multiverse can be connected, but it turns out that the boundary of a black hole is similar in important ways to the so-called cosmological horizon–the boundary of the space-time region within which we can receive signals from deep space. The horizon exists because space is expanding exponentially, and objects farther than this cutoff are receding faster than the speed of light, so any message from them can never reach us. The situation, therefore, is akin to a black hole viewed by a distant observer. Also, as in the case of the black hole, quantum mechanics requires an observer inside the horizon to view space-time on the other side of the boundary–in this case, the exterior of the cosmological horizon–as nonexistent. If we consider such space-time in addition to the information that can be retrieved from the horizon later (analogous to Hawking radiation in the black hole case), then we are overcounting the information. This problem implies that any description of the quantum state of the universe should include only the region within (and on) the horizon–in particular, there can be no infinite space in any single, consistent description of the cosmos.

If a quantum state reflects only the region within the horizon, then where is the multiverse, which we thought existed in an eternally inflating infinite space? The answer is that the creation of bubble universes is probabilistic, like any other process in quantum mechanics. Just as a quantum measurement could spawn many different results distinguished by their probability of occurring, inflation could produce many different universes, each with a different probability of coming into being. In other words, the quantum state representing eternally inflating space is a superposition of worlds–or branches–representing different universes, with each of these branches including only the region within its own horizon.

Because each of these universes is finite, we avoid the problem of predictability that was raised by the prospect of an infinitely large space that encompasses all possible outcomes. The multiple universes in this case do not all exist simultaneously in real space–they coexist only in "probability space," that is, as possible outcomes of observations made by people living inside each world. Thus, each universe–each possible outcome–retains a specific probability of coming into being.

This picture unifies the eternally inflating multiverse of cosmology and Everett's many worlds. Cosmic history then unfolds like this: the multiverse starts from some initial state and evolves into a superposition of many bubble universes. As time passes, the states representing each of these bubbles further branch into more superpositions of states representing the various possible outcomes of "experiments" performed within those universes (these need not be scientific experiments–they can be any physical processes). Eventually the state representing the whole multiverse will thus contain an enormous number of branches, each of which represents a possible world that may arise from the initial state. Quantum-mechanical probabilities therefore determine outcomes in cosmology and in microscopic processes. The multiverse and quantum many worlds are really the same thing; they simply refer to the same phenomenon–superposition–occurring at vastly different scales.

In this new picture, our world is only one of all possible worlds that are allowed by the fundamental principles of quantum physics and that exist simultaneously in probability space.

The Realm Beyond

To know if this idea is correct, we would want to test it experimentally. But is that feasible? It turns out that discovery of one particular phenomenon would lend support to the new thinking. The multiverse could lead to a small amount of negative spatial curvature in our universe–in other words, objects would travel through space not along straight lines as in a flat cosmos but along curves, even in the absence of gravity. Such curvature could happen because, even though the bubble universes are finite as seen from the perspective of the entire multiverse, observers inside a bubble would perceive their universe to be infinitely large, which would make space seem negatively curved (an example of negative curvature is the surface of a saddle, whereas the surface of a sphere is positively curved). If we were inside one such bubble, space should likewise appear to us to be bent.

Evidence so far indicates that the cosmos is flat, but experiments studying how distant light bends as it travels through the cosmos are likely to improve measures of the curvature of our universe by about two orders of magnitude in the next few decades. If these experiments find any amount of negative curvature, they will support the multiverse concept because, although such curvature is technically possible in a single universe, it is implausible there. Specifically, a discovery supports the quantum multiverse picture described here because it can naturally lead to curvature large enough to be detected, whereas the traditional inflationary picture of the multiverse tends to produce negative curvature many orders of magnitude smaller than we can hope to measure.

Interestingly, the discovery of positive curvature would falsify the multiverse notion presented here because inflation theory suggests that bubble universes could produce only negative curvature. On the other hand, if we are lucky, we may even see dramatic signs of a multiverse–such as a remnant from a "collision" of bubble universes in the sky, which may be formed in a single branch in the quantum multiverse. Scientists are, however, far from certain that we will ever detect such signals.

I and other physicists are also pursuing the quantum multiverse idea further on a theoretical level. We can ask fundamental questions such as: How can we determine the quantum state of the entire multiverse? What is time, and how does it emerge? The quantum multiverse picture does not immediately answer these questions, but it does provide a framework to address them. Lately, for instance, I have found that constraints imposed by the mathematical requirement that our theory must include rigorously defined probabilities may enable us to determine the unique quantum state of the entire multiverse. These constraints also suggest that the overall quantum state stays constant even though a physical observer, who is a part of the multiverse state, will see that new bubbles constantly form. This implies that our sense of the universe changing over time and, indeed, the concept of time itself may be an illusion. Time, according to this notion, is an "emergent concept" that arises from a more fundamental reality and seems to exist only within local branches of the multiverse.

Many of the ideas I have discussed are still quite speculative, but it is thrilling that physicists can talk about such big and deep questions based on theoretical progress. Who knows where these explorations will finally lead us? It seems clear, though, that we live in an exciting era in which our scientific explorations reach beyond what we thought to be the entire physical world—our universe—into a potentially limitless realm.

About the Author

Yasunori Nomura is a professor of physics and director of the Berkeley Center for Theoretical Physics at the University of California, Berkeley. He is also a senior faculty scientist at Lawrence Berkeley National Laboratory and a principal investigator at the University of Tokyo's Kavli Institute for the Physics and Mathematics of the Universe.

Space: The Final Illusion

By Lee Smolin

Many of the great advances in science are marked by the discovery that an aspect of nature we thought was fundamental is actually an illusion, the result of the coarseness of our sensory perceptions. Thus, air and water appear to us to be continuous fluids, but we discover on deeper experiment that they are made of atoms. Earth appears to us motionless, but a deeper understanding teaches us that it moves relative to the sun and the galaxy.

One persistent illusion is that physical objects interact only with other objects they are close to. This is called the principle of locality. We can express this idea more precisely by the law that the strength of forces between any two objects falls off quickly—at least by some power of the distance between them. This can be explained by positing that the bodies interact not directly but only through the mediation of a field, such as an electromagnetic field, which propagates from one body to the other. Fields spread out as they propagate, with the field lines covering a constantly greater area—providing a natural explanation for the laws that say the forces between charges and masses fall off by the square of the distance between them.

Locality is an aspect of an even more compelling illusion: that we exist within an absolute space, with respect to which we mark our positions as we move "through" it. Thus, Isaac Newton opined that motion is ultimately defined as change of position with respect to absolute space. If this seems obscure—because no measurement can establish a relation of a physical object to this imagined absolute space—Newton assured us that absolute space is seen by God, making your location relative to it an aspect of the divinity of the world. We humans must make do with relative positions and motions—which are defined relative to physical objects we can see.

Gottfried Wilhelm Leibniz broke the mystification by declaring that all that exists is relative positions and motions. He proposed as a matter of principle that any acceptable science of motion must be formulated in terms of relative motions alone. And this, after two centuries of waiting, is what Albert Einstein delivered to us in his general theory of relativity. In this glorious construction, space is subsumed into space-time, which is explicable as a dynamically evolving network of relations.

And what defines those relations? Nothing but causality. The elements of space-time are events–the ultimate expression of locality–and each of these is caused by events in their past. Each event will also become a cause of events in the future. Most of the information in the geometry of space-time is actually a coding of the relations of causality that relate the events.

Thus, we see that the idea that physical forces must act locally is a consequence of a deeper principle, which is that physical effects have causal processes. And the basic principles of relativity theory insist that causes can propagate through space only at finite speeds, which cannot exceed the speed of light. We call this the principle of relativistic causality.

This principle would seem to be so natural that it must be true. But not so fast. Of all the strange aspects of quantum physics so far discovered, the strangest of all has to be the shocking discovery that the principle of relativistic causality is violated by quantum phenomena. Roughly speaking, if two particles interact and then separate, flying far apart from each other, they nonetheless may continue to share properties of a strange kind, that may be ascribed to the pair, without each of the individuals having themselves any definite properties. We say the two particles are "entangled."

When two particles are in such an entangled state, an experimenter can, it turns out, affect the properties of one of the particles, directly and immediately, by choosing to measure some particular corresponding property of the other. It matters not at all that it would require a signal much faster than light to directly effect such an influence.

This has been shown in many experiments carried out since the 1970s, which test a notion of locality formulated by John Bell in 1964—and all the results show that entangled pairs violate that concept of locality.

In its present form, quantum mechanics predicts only statistical averages for the outcomes of many kinds of experiments, including these. Consequently, it is not possible to use the nonlocality present in entangled pairs to send a signal faster than light. But many physicists, in an ambition going back to Einstein, Louis de Broglie, Erwin Schrödinger and the other inventors of quantum mechanics, aspire to discover an improved version of quantum theory.

This would go deeper and replace the present statistical theory with a more complete theory, which would provide a complete and exact description of what goes on in every individual quantum process. For such a theory to work, it would have to be based on influences traveling arbitrarily faster than light, thus destroying the principle of relativistic causality, as well as our intuitive notions of local influence.

Is such a more complete understanding of quantum physics possible? And how are we to search for it? I believe it is not only possible but an inevitable next step in the progress of physics. I believe that the completion of quantum mechanics will be a major part of the resolution of another deep problem—that of unifying our understandings of gravity, space-time and the quantum, to produce a quantum theory of gravity.

The reason is that there is good evidence that the quantum theory of gravity will itself engender big violations of locality. And as Fotini Markopoulou, then at the Perimeter Institute, and I first proposed in 2003, the violations of locality forced on us by quantum gravity are precisely what are needed to explain the nonlocality brought on by quantum entanglement.

If we are to have a complete physics, we must unify the geometrical picture of space-time given by general relativity with quantum physics. There is some theoretical evidence that this project of making a quantum theory of gravity will require space and space-time to become discrete and built out of finite atoms of geometry.

In the same sense that a liquid is just a description of the collective motions of myriads of atoms, space and space-time will turn out to be just a way of talking about the collective properties of the large number of atomic events. Their constant coming in and out of being, causing the next ones as they recede into the past, make up the continual construction of the world–also known to us as the flow of time.

The aim of a quantum theory of gravity is then first to hypothesize the laws that govern the elementary events, by which they continually come into being and then recede into the past. Then we must show how a large-scale picture emerges, in which these discrete events become subsumed in an emergent description of a smooth and continuous space-time–as described by Einstein's 1915 general theory of relativity.

Initially there is no space–just a network of individual elementary events, together with the relations expressing which of these were the direct causes of which other events. The notion of the flow of events collectively giving rise to a smooth description in terms of the geometry of a space-time must emerge–and the most important aspect of this is locality. The notion of distance must emerge and in such a way that those events that are close to each other are, on average, correspondingly more likely to have influenced each other. Getting this right is the holy grail for quantum gravity theorists.

Notice that if this is right, there are two notions of locality: a fundamental locality, which is based on the actual facts of which fundamental events were causes of which, and an approximate, collective, emergent notion of which events are near to each other in space and space-time. The familiar macroscopic notion of distance is then based on a collective averaging of all the myriad fundamental causal processes. To get a sense of how much is involved in this average, we expect that during each second there are around 10120 elementary events happening within each cubic centimeter of space.

Indeed, one way to approach quantum gravity is to aim to derive the Einstein equations, which are the laws general relativity applies to space-time, from the laws of thermodynamics, applied to countless elementary events. This strategy was introduced in 1995 by Ted

Jacobson of the University of Maryland, College Park, in one of the few papers admired by quantum gravity theorists of all stripes.

But here we get a surprise and, quite possibly, an opportunity. For the collective, large-scale notion of nearness is meant to correspond to the fundamental notion of causality when averaged over vast numbers of events. This gives the individual fundamental events and their causal relations a great deal of freedom to depart from the averages.

For example, let us pick just two elementary events, one in the cup of coffee you are now drinking and the other in a cup of whatever it is they drink on one of the planets of Proxima Centauri. These events may be separated by four light-years—but nothing prevents one from being an elementary cause of the other.

We can choose these two events so that they are nearly simultaneous as we (or the Proximas) measure time. Thus, it violates the principles of Einstein's theories of relativity to have one of these events be the cause of the other. But there need not be a contradiction if we regard the laws of relativity as emergent regularities to govern the collective large-scale average. This is just how we regard the laws of thermodynamics as arising from averages over large collections of atoms, whose individuals follow different laws.

When a law emerges from a statistical averaging, there are always relatively rare events in which individual atoms violate the rule that holds on average. We call these fluctuations. A good example is the tendency of collections of atoms, when cooled, to form regular crystal patterns. But from time to time an atom ends up in the wrong place, disrupting the beautiful symmetry of the crystal arrangement. We say the pattern has been disordered.

I can then summarize the story I've been telling by saying that when locality, and space itself, emerges from averaging over fundamental processes involving a myriad of individual events, it is inevitable that locality will be disordered. Mostly, influences will be local because most of the time, causally related events will end up close to each other in the emergent rough description we call space. But there will be many pairs of events that are causally related but that will end up far from each other–thus disordering space and locality.

Could this disordering of locality serve to explain the quantum nonlocality inherent in entangled particles? I believe the answer is yes. Indeed, we have shown this to be the case in two different models of fundamental completions of quantum mechanics.

The details are unimportant, especially at this early stage. But the takeaway lesson is that the intuitive idea that objects influence each other because they are close in space is soon to become another of those easy beliefs that turn out to be wrong when we look deeper. The smoothness of space is soon to become an illusion that hides a tiny and complex world of causal interactions, which do not live in space–but which rather define and create space as they create the future from the present.

About the Author

Lee Smolin is a senior and founding faculty member at the Perimeter Institute for Theoretical Physics in Waterloo, Ontario, and adjunct professor of physics at the University of Waterloo. In addition to his work on quantum gravity, he is interested in elementary particle physics, cosmology and the foundation of quantum theory. His latest book is Einstein's Unfinished Revolution, *published in 2019 by Penguin.*

What Is Space-Time Really Made Of?

By Adam Becker

Natalie Paquette spends her time thinking about how to grow an extra dimension. Start with little circles, scattered across every point in space and time–a curlicue dimension, looped back onto itself. Then shrink those circles down, smaller and smaller, tightening the loop, until a curious transformation occurs: the dimension stops seeming tiny and instead becomes enormous, like when you realize something that looks small and nearby is actually huge and distant. "We're shrinking a spatial direction," Paquette says. "But when we try to shrink it past a certain point, a new, large spatial direction emerges instead."

Paquette, a theoretical physicist at the University of Washington, is not alone in thinking about this strange kind of dimensional transmutation. A growing number of physicists, working in different areas of the discipline with different approaches, are increasingly converging on a profound idea: space–and perhaps even time–is not fundamental. Instead space and time may be *emergent*: they could arise from the structure and behavior of more basic components of nature. At the deepest level of reality, questions like "Where?" and "When?" simply may not have answers at all. "We have a lot of hints from physics that space-time as we understand it isn't the fundamental thing," Paquette says.

These radical notions come from the latest twists in the century-long hunt for a theory of quantum gravity. Physicists' best theory of gravity is general relativity, Albert Einstein's famous conception of how matter warps space and time. Their best theory of everything else is quantum physics, which is astonishingly accurate when it comes to the properties of matter, energy and subatomic particles. Both theories have easily passed all the tests physicists have been able to devise for the past century. Put them together, one might think, and you would have a "theory of everything."

But the two theories don't play nicely. Ask general relativity what happens in the context of quantum physics, and you'll get contradictory answers, with untamed infinities breaking loose across your calculations. Nature knows how to apply gravity in quantum contexts–it happened in the first moments of the big bang, and it still happens in the hearts of black holes–but we humans are still struggling to understand how the trick is done. Part of the problem lies in the ways the two theories deal with space and time. While quantum physics treats space and time as immutable, general relativity warps them for breakfast.

Somehow a theory of quantum gravity would need to reconcile these ideas about space and time. One way to do that would be to eliminate the problem at its source, space-time itself, by making space and time emerge from something more fundamental. In recent years several different lines of inquiry have all suggested that, at the deepest level of reality, space and time do not exist in the same way that they do in our everyday world. Over the past decade these ideas have radically changed how physicists think about black holes. Now researchers are using these concepts to elucidate the workings of something even more exotic: wormholes–hypothetical tunnel-like connections between distant points in space-time. These successes have kept alive the hope of an even deeper breakthrough. If space-time is emergent, then figuring out where it comes from–and how it could arise from anything else–may just be the missing key that finally unlocks the door to a theory of everything.

The World in a String Duet

Today the most popular candidate theory of quantum gravity among physicists is string theory. According to this idea, its eponymous strings are the fundamental constituents of matter and energy, giving rise to the myriad fundamental subatomic particles seen at particle accelerators around the world. They are even responsible for gravity–a hypothetical particle that carries the gravitational force, a "graviton," is an inevitable consequence of the theory.

But string theory is difficult to understand–it lives in mathematical territory that has taken physicists and mathematicians decades to explore. Much of the theory's structure is still uncharted, expeditions still planned and maps left to be made. Within this new realm, the main technique for navigation is through mathematical dualities–correspondences between one kind of system and another.

One example is the duality from the beginning of this article, between tiny dimensions and big ones. Try to cram a dimension down into a little space, and string theory tells you that you will end up with something mathematically identical to a world where that dimension is huge instead. The two situations are the same, according to string theory–you can go back and forth from one to the other freely and use techniques from one situation to understand how the other one works. "If you carefully keep track of the fundamental building blocks of the theory," Paquette says, "you can naturally find sometimes that ... you might grow a new spatial dimension."

A similar duality suggests to many string theorists that space itself is emergent. The idea began in 1997, when Juan Maldacena, a physicist at the Institute for Advanced Study, uncovered a duality between a kind of well-understood quantum theory known as a conformal field theory (CFT) and a special kind of space-time from general relativity known as anti–de Sitter space (AdS). The two seem to be wildly different theories–the CFT has no gravity in it whatsoever, and the AdS space has all of Einstein's theory of gravity thrown in. Yet the same mathematics can describe both worlds. When it was discovered, this AdS/CFT correspondence provided a tangible mathematical link between a quantum theory and a full universe with gravity in it.

Curiously, the AdS space in the AdS/CFT correspondence had one more dimension in it than the quantum CFT had. But physicists relished this mismatch because it was a fully worked-out example of another kind of correspondence conceived a few years earlier, from physicists Gerard 't Hooft of Utrecht University in the Netherlands and Leonard Susskind of Stanford University, known as the holographic principle. Based on some of the peculiar characteristics of black holes, 't Hooft and Susskind suspected that the properties of a region of space might be fully "encoded" by its boundary. In other words, the two-dimensional surface of a black hole would contain all the information needed to know what was in its three-dimensional interior–like a hologram. "I think a lot of people thought we were nuts," Susskind says. "Two good physicists gone bad."

Similarly, in the AdS/CFT correspondence, the four-dimensional CFT encodes everything about the five-dimensional AdS space it is associated with. In this system, the entire region of space-time is built out of interactions between the components of the quantum system in the conformal field theory. Maldacena likens this process to reading a novel. "If you are telling a story in a book, there are the characters in the book that are doing something," he says. "But all there is is a line of text, right? What the characters are doing is inferred from this line of text. The characters in the book would be like the bulk [AdS] theory. And the line of text is the [CFT]."

But where does the space in the AdS space come from? If this space is emergent, what is it emerging from? The answer is a special and strangely quantum kind of interaction in the CFT: entanglement, a long-distance connection between objects, instantaneously correlating their behavior in statistically improbable ways. Entanglement famously troubled Einstein, who called it "spooky action at a distance."

Yet despite its spookiness, entanglement is a core feature of quantum physics. When any two objects interact in quantum mechanics, they generally become entangled and will stay entangled so long as they remain isolated from the rest of the world–no matter how far apart they may travel. In experiments, physicists have maintained entanglement between particles more than 1,000 kilometers apart and even between particles on the ground and others sent to orbiting satellites. In principle, two entangled particles could sustain their connection on opposite sides of the galaxy or the universe. Distance simply does not seem to matter for entanglement, a puzzle that has troubled many physicists for decades.

But if space is emergent, entanglement's ability to persist over large distances might not be terribly mysterious–after all, distance is a construct. According to studies of the AdS/CFT correspondence by physicists Shinsei Ryu of Princeton University and Tadashi Takayanagi of Kyoto University, entanglement is what produces distances in the AdS space in the first place. Any two nearby regions of space on the AdS side of the duality correspond to two highly entangled quantum components of the CFT. The more entangled they are, the closer together the regions of space are.

In recent years physicists have come to suspect that this relation might apply to our universe as well. "What is it that holds the space together and keeps it from falling apart into separate subregions? The answer is the entanglement between two parts of space," Susskind says. "The continuity and the connectivity of space owes its existence to quantum-mechanical entanglement." Entanglement, then, may undergird the structure of space itself, forming the warp and weft that give rise to the geometry of the world. "If you could somehow destroy the entanglement between two parts [of space], the space would fall apart," Susskind says. "It would do the opposite of emerging. It would dis-emerge."

If space is made of entanglement, then the puzzle of quantum gravity seems much easier to solve: instead of trying to account for the warping of space in a quantum way, space itself emerges out of a fundamentally quantum phenomenon. Susskind suspects this is why a theory of quantum gravity has been so difficult to find in the first place. "I think the reason it never worked very well is because it started with a picture of two different things, [general relativity] and quantum mechanics, and put them together," he says. "And I think the point is really that they're much too closely related to pull apart and then put back together again. There's no such thing as gravity without quantum mechanics."

Yet accounting for emergent space is only half the job. With space and time so intimately linked in relativity, any account of how space emerges must also explain time. "Time must also emerge somehow," says Mark van Raamsdonk, a physicist at the University of British Columbia and a pioneer in the connection between entanglement and space-time. "But this is not well understood and is an active area of research."

Another active area, he says, is using models of emergent space-time to understand wormholes. Previously many physicists had believed that sending objects through a wormhole was impossible, even in theory. But in the past few years physicists working on the AdS/CFT correspondence and similar models have found new ways to construct wormholes. "We don't know if we could do that in our universe," van Raamsdonk says. "But what we now know is that certain kinds of traversable wormholes are theoretically possible." Two papers–one in 2016 and one in 2018–led to an ongoing flurry of work in the area. But even if traversable wormholes could be built, they would not be much use for space travel. As Susskind points out, "you can't go through that wormhole faster than it would take for [light] to go the long way around."

Space to Think

If the string theorists are correct, then space is built from quantum entanglement, and time might be as well. But what would that really mean? How can space be "made of" entanglement between objects unless those objects are themselves somewhere? How can those objects become entangled unless they experience time and change? And what kind of existence could things have without inhabiting a true space and time?

These are questions verging on philosophy–and indeed, philosophers of physics are taking them seriously. "How the hell could space-time be the kind of thing that could be emergent?" asks Eleanor Knox, a philosopher of physics at King's College London. Intuitively, she says, that seems impossible. But Knox doesn't think that is a problem. "Our intuitions are terrible sometimes," she says. They "evolved on the African savanna interacting with macro objects and macro fluids and biological animals" and tend not to transfer to the world of quantum mechanics. When it comes to quantum gravity, " 'Where's the stuff?' and 'Where does it live?' aren't the right questions to be asking," Knox concludes.

It is certainly true that objects live in places in everyday life. But as Knox and many others point out, that does not mean that space and time have to be fundamental–just that they have to reliably emerge from whatever is fundamental. Consider a liquid, says Christian Wüthrich, a philosopher of physics at the University of Geneva. "Ultimately it's elementary particles, like electrons and protons and neutrons or, even more fundamental, quarks and leptons. Do quarks and leptons have liquid properties? That just doesn't make sense, right?... Nevertheless, when these fundamental particles come together in sufficient numbers and show a certain behavior together, collective behavior, then they will act in a way that is like a liquid."

Space and time, Wüthrich says, could work the same way in string theory and other theories of quantum gravity. Specifically, space-time might emerge from the materials we usually think of as living in the universe–matter and energy itself. "It's not [that] we first have space and time and then we add in some matter," Wüthrich says. "Rather something material may be a necessary condition for there to be space and time. That's still a very close connection, but it's just the other way from what you might have thought originally."

But there are other ways to interpret the latest findings. The AdS/CFT correspondence is often seen as an example of how space-time might emerge from a quantum system, but that might not actually be what it shows, according to Alyssa Ney, a philosopher of physics at the University of California, Davis. "AdS/CFT gives you this ability to provide a translation manual between facts about the space-time and facts of the quantum theory," Ney says. "That's compatible with the claim that space-time is emergent, and some quantum theory is fundamental." But the reverse is also true, she says. The correspondence could mean that quantum theory is emergent and space-time is fundamental–or that neither is fundamental and that there is some even deeper fundamental theory out there. Emergence is a strong claim to make, Ney says, and she is open to the possibility that it is true. "But at least just looking at AdS/CFT, I'm still not seeing a clear argument for emergence."

An arguably bigger challenge to the string theory picture of emergent space-time is hidden in plain sight, right in the name of the AdS/CFT correspondence itself. "We don't live in anti–de Sitter space," Susskind says. "We live in something much closer to de Sitter space." De Sitter space describes an accelerating and expanding universe much like our own. "We haven't got the vaguest idea how [holography] applies there," Susskind concludes. Figuring out how to set up this kind of correspondence for a space that more closely resembles the actual universe is one of the most pressing problems for string theorists. "I think we're going to be able to understand better how to get into a cosmological version of this," van Raamsdonk says.

Finally, there is the news—or lack thereof—from the latest particle accelerators, which have not found any evidence for the extra particles predicted by supersymmetry, an idea that string theory relies on. Supersymmetry dictates that all known particles would have their own "superpartners," doubling the number of fundamental particles. But CERN's Large Hadron Collider near Geneva, designed in part to search for superpartners, has seen no sign of them. "All of the really precise versions of [emergent space-time] that we have are in supersymmetric theories," Susskind says. "Once you don't have supersymmetry, the ability to mathematically follow the equations just evaporates out of your hands."

Atoms of Space-Time

String theory is not the only idea that suggests space-time is emergent. String theory has "failed to live up to [its] promise as a way to unite gravity and quantum mechanics," says Abhay Ashtekar, a physicist at Pennsylvania State University. "The power of string theory now is in providing an extremely rich set of tools, which has been used widely across the whole spectrum of physics." Ashtekar is one of the original pioneers of the most popular alternative to string theory, known as loop quantum gravity. In loop quantum gravity, space and time are not smooth and continuous the way they are in general relativity–instead they are made of discrete components, what Ashtekar calls "chunks or atoms of space-time."

These atoms of space-time are connected in a network, with one- and two-dimensional surfaces joining them together into what practitioners of loop quantum gravity call a spin foam. And despite that foam being limited to two dimensions, it gives rise to our four-dimensional world, with three dimensions of space and one of time. Ashtekar likens it to a piece of clothing. "If you look at your shirt, it looks like a two-dimensional surface," he says. "If you just take a magnifying glass, you will immediately see that it's all one-dimensional threads. It's just that those threads are so densely packed that for all practical purposes, you can think of the shirt as being a two-dimensional surface. So, similarly, the space around us looks like a three-dimensional continuum. But there is really a crisscross by these [atoms of space-time]."

Although string theory and loop quantum gravity both suggest that space-time is emergent, the kind of emergence is different in the two theories. String theory suggests that space-time (or at least space) emerges from the behavior of a seemingly unrelated system, in the form of entanglement. Think of how traffic jams emerge from the collective decisions of individual drivers. The cars are not made of traffic–the cars make the traffic. In loop quantum gravity, on the other hand, the emergence of space-time is more like a sloping sand dune emerging from the collective motion of sand grains in wind. The smooth familiar space-time comes from the collective behavior of tiny "grains" of space-time; like the dunes, the grains are still sand, even though the chunky crystalline grains do not look or act like the undulating dunes.

Despite these differences, both loop quantum gravity and string theory suggest space-time emerges from some underlying reality. Nor are they the only proposed theories of quantum gravity that point in this direction. Causal set theory, another contender for a theory of quantum gravity, posits that space and time are made of more fundamental components as well. "It's really striking that for most of the plausible theories of quantum gravity that we have, in some sense their message is, yeah, general relativistic space-time isn't in there at the fundamental level," Knox says. "People get very excited when different theories of quantum gravity agree on at least something."

The Future of Space at the Edge of Time

Modern physics is a victim of its own success. Because quantum physics and general relativity are both so phenomenally accurate, quantum gravity is needed only to describe extreme situations, when enormous masses are stuffed into unfathomably tiny spaces. Those conditions exist in only a few places in nature, such as the center of a black hole–and notably not in physics laboratories, not even the largest and most powerful ones. It would take a particle accelerator the size of a galaxy to directly test the behavior of nature under conditions where quantum gravity reigns. This lack of direct experimental data is a large part of the reason why scientists' search for a theory of quantum gravity has been so long.

Faced with the lack of evidence, most physicists have pinned their hopes on the sky. In the earliest moments of the big bang, the entire universe was phenomenally small and dense–a situation that calls for quantum gravity to describe it. And echoes of that era may remain in the sky today. "I think our best bet [for testing quantum gravity] is through cosmology," Maldacena says. "Maybe something in cosmology that we now think is unpredictable, that maybe can be predicted once we understand the full theory, or some new thing that we didn't even think about."

Laboratory experiments may come in handy, however, for testing string theory, at least indirectly. Scientists hope to study the AdS/CFT correspondence not by probing space-time but by building highly entangled systems of atoms and seeing whether an analogue to space-time and gravity shows up in their behavior. Such experiments might "have some features of gravity, though, perhaps not all the features," Maldacena says. "It also depends on exactly what you call gravity."

Will we ever know the real nature of space and time? The observational data from the skies may not be forthcoming any time soon. The lab experiments could be a bust. And as philosophers know well, questions about the true nature of space and time are very old indeed. What exists "is now all together, one, continuous," said the philosopher Parmenides 2,500 years ago. "All is full of what is." Parmenides insisted that time and change were illusions, that everything everywhere was one and the same. His pupil Zeno created famous paradoxes to prove his teacher's point, purporting to show that motion over any distance was impossible. Their work raised the question of whether time and space are somehow illusory, an unsettling prospect that has haunted Western philosophy for over two millennia.

"The fact that the ancient Greeks asked things like, 'What is space?' 'What is time?' 'What is change?' and that we still ask versions of these questions today means that they were the right questions to ask," Wüthrich says. "It's by thinking about these kinds of questions that we have learned a lot about physics."

About the Author

Adam Becker is a science writer at Lawrence Berkeley National Laboratory and author of What Is Real?, *about the sordid untold history of quantum physics. His writing has appeared in the* New York Times, *the BBC, and elsewhere. He earned a Ph.D. in cosmology from the University of Michigan.*

Can We Gauge Quantum Time of Flight?

By Anil Ananthaswamy

A deceptively simple experiment that involves making precise measurements of the time it takes for a particle to go from point A to point B could cause a breakthrough in quantum physics. The findings could focus attention on an alternative to standard quantum theory called Bohmian mechanics, which posits an underworld of unseen waves that guide particles from place to place.

A new study, by a team at the Ludwig Maximilian University of Munich (L.M.U.) in Germany, makes precise predictions for such an experiment using Bohmian mechanics, a theory formulated by theoretical physicist David Bohm in the 1950s and augmented by modern-day theorists. Standard quantum theory fails in this regard, and physicists have to resort to assumptions and approximations to calculate particle transit times. "If people knew that a theory that they love so much–standard quantum mechanics–cannot make [precise] predictions in such a simple case, that should at least make them wonder," says theorist and L.M.U. team member Serj Aristarhov.

It is no secret that the quantum world is weird. Consider a setup in which an electron gun fires the subatomic particles at a screen, as in the classic "double-slit experiment." You cannot predict exactly where any given electron will land to form, say, a fluorescent dot. But you can predict with precision the spatial distribution, or pattern, of dots that takes shape over time as the electrons land one by one. Some locations will have more electrons; others will have fewer. But this weirdness hides something even stranger. All else being equal, each electron will reach the detector at a slightly different time, its so-called arrival time. Just like the positions, the arrival times will have a distribution: some arrival times will be more common, and others will be less so. Textbook quantum physics has no mechanism for precisely predicting this temporal distribution. "Normal quantum theory is concerned only with 'where'; they ignore the 'when,'" says team member and theorist Siddhant Das. "That's one way to diagnose that there's something fishy."

There is a deep reason for this curious shortcoming. In standard quantum theory, a physical property that can be measured is called an observable. The position of a particle, for example, is an observable. Each and every observable is associated with a corresponding mathematical entity called an operator. But the standard theory has no such operator for observing time. In 1933 Austrian theoretical physicist Wolfgang Pauli showed that quantum theory could not accommodate a time operator, at least not in the standard way of thinking about it. "We conclude therefore that the introduction of a time operator ... must be abandoned fundamentally," he wrote.

Yet measuring particle arrival times, or their "time of flight," is an important part of experimental physics. Detectors at CERN's Large Hadron Collider, for example, and instruments called mass spectrometers use such measurements to calculate the masses and momenta of particles, ions and molecules. There is, however, a serious wrinkle: although these calculations concern quantum systems, they cannot be made using unadulterated quantum mechanics. Instead they require assumptions. In one method, for example, experimenters assume that once the particle leaves its source, it behaves classically, meaning it follows Newton's equations of motion.

The result is a hybrid approach–one that is part quantum, part classical. It starts with the quantum perspective, in which each particle is represented by a mathematical abstraction called a wave function. Identically prepared particles will have identical wave functions when they are released from their source. But measuring the momentum of each particle (or, for that matter, its position) at the instant of release will yield different values each time. Taken together, these values follow a distribution that is precisely predicted by the initial wave function. Starting from this ensemble of values for identically prepared particles and assuming that a particle follows a classical trajectory once it is emitted, the result is a distribution of arrival times at the detector that depends on the initial momentum distribution.

Standard theory is also often used for another quantum-mechanical method for calculating arrival times. As a particle flies toward a detector, its wave function evolves according to the Schrödinger equation, which describes a particle's changing state over time. Consider the one-dimensional case of a detector that is a certain horizontal distance from an emission source. The Schrödinger equation determines the wave function of the particle–and hence the probability of detecting that particle at that location–assuming that the particle crosses the location only once. (There is, of course, no clear way to substantiate this assumption in standard quantum mechanics.) Using such assumptions, physicists can calculate the probability that the particle will arrive at the detector at a given time (t) or earlier. "From the perspective of standard quantum mechanics, it sounds perfectly fine," Aristarhov says. "And you expect to have a nice answer from that."

There is a hitch, however. To go from the probability that the arrival time is less than or equal to t to the probability that it is exactly equal to t involves calculating a quantity that physicists call the quantum flux, or quantum probability current–a measure of how the probability of finding the particle at the detector location changes with time. This works well, except that at times the quantum flux can be negative. Even though it is hard to find wave functions for which the quantity becomes appreciably negative, nothing "prohibits this quantity from being negative," Aristarhov says. "And this is a disaster." A negative quantum flux leads to negative probabilities, and probabilities can never be less than zero.

Using the Schrödinger evolution to calculate the distribution of arrival times works only when the quantum flux is positive–a case that, in the real world, only definitively exists when the detector is in the "far field," or at a considerable distance from the source, and the particle is moving freely in the absence of potentials. When experimentalists measure such far-field arrival times, both the hybrid and quantum-flux approaches make similar predictions that tally well with experimental findings. But they do not make clear predictions for "near field" cases, where the detector is very close to the source.

Bohmian Predictions

In 2018 Das and Aristarhov, along with their then Ph.D. adviser Detlef Dürr, an expert on Bohmian mechanics at L.M.U., who died in 2021, began working with colleagues on Bohmian-based predictions of arrival times. Bohm's theory holds that each particle is guided by its wave function. Unlike standard quantum mechanics, in which a particle is considered to have no precise position or momentum prior to a measurement–and hence no trajectory–particles in Bohmian mechanics are real and have squiggly trajectories described by precise equations of motion (albeit ones that differ from Newton's equations of motion).

Among the researchers' first findings was that far-field measurements would fail to distinguish between the predictions of Bohmian mechanics and those of the hybrid or quantum-flux approaches. This is because over large distances Bohmian trajectories become straight lines, so the hybrid semiclassical approximation holds. Also, for straight far-field trajectories, the quantum flux is always positive, and its value is predicted exactly by Bohmian mechanics. "If you put a detector far enough [away] and you do Bohmian analysis, you see that it coincides with the hybrid approach and the quantum-flux approach," Aristarhov says.

The key, then, is to do near-field measurements–but those have long been considered impossible. "The near-field regime is very volatile," Das says. "It's very sensitive to the initial wave-function shape you have created." Also, "if you come very close to the region of initial preparation, the particle will just be detected instantaneously. You cannot resolve [the arrival times] and see the differences between this prediction and that prediction."

To avoid this problem, Das and Dürr proposed an experimental setup that would allow particles to be detected far away from the source while still generating unique results that could distinguish the predictions of Bohmian mechanics from those of the more standard methods.

Conceptually, the team's proposed setup is simple. Imagine a waveguide–a cylindrical pathway that confines the motion of a particle (an optical fiber is such a waveguide for photons of light, for example). On one end of the waveguide, prepare a particle–ideally an electron or some particle of matter–in its lowest energy, or ground, state and trap it in a bowl-shaped electric potential well. This well is actually the composite of two adjacent potential barriers that collectively create the parabolic shape. If one of the barriers is switched off, the particle will still be blocked by the other that remains in place, but it is free to escape from the well into the waveguide.

Das pursued the painstaking task of fleshing out the experiment's parameters, performing calculations and simulations to determine the theoretical distribution of arrival times at a detector placed far away from a source along a waveguide's axis. After a few years of work, he had obtained clear results for two different types of initial wave functions associated with particles such as electrons. Each wave function can be characterized by something called its spin vector. Imagine an arrow associated with the wave function that can be pointing in any direction. The team looked at two cases: one in which the arrow points along the axis of the waveguide and another in which it is perpendicular to that axis.

The team showed that when the wave function's spin vector is aligned along the waveguide's axis, the distribution of arrival times predicted by the quantum-flux method is identical to that predicted by Bohmian mechanics. But these distributions differ significantly from those calculated for the hybrid approach. When the spin vector is perpendicular, the distinctions become even starker. With help from their L.M.U. colleague Markus Nöth, the researchers showed that all the Bohmian trajectories will strike the detector at or before this cutoff time. "This was very unexpected," Das says.

Again, the Bohmian prediction differs significantly from the predictions of the semiclassical hybrid theory, which do not exhibit such a sharp arrival-time cutoff. And crucially, in this scenario, the quantum flux is negative, meaning that calculating arrival times using Schrödinger evolution becomes impossible. The standard quantum theorists "put their hands up when [the quantum flux] becomes negative," Das says. But Bohmian mechanics continues to make predictions. "There's a clear distinction between [it] and everything else," Aristarhov says.

Experimentalists Enter the Fray

Quantum theorist Charis Anastopoulos of the University of Patras in Greece, an expert on arrival times, who was not involved with this work, is both impressed and circumspect. "The setup they are proposing seems plausible," he says. And because each approach to calculating the distribution of arrival times involves a different way of thinking about quantum reality, a clear experimental finding could jolt the foundations of quantum mechanics. "It will vindicate particular ways of thinking," Anastopoulos says. "So in this way, it will have some impact.... If it [agrees with] Bohmian mechanics, which is a very distinctive prediction, this would be a great impact, of course."

At least one experimentalist is gearing up to make the team's proposal a reality. Before Dürr's death, Ferdinand Schmidt-Kaler of the Johannes Gutenberg University Mainz in Germany had been in discussions with him about testing arrival times. Schmidt-Kaler is an expert on a type of ion trap in which electric fields are used to confine a single calcium ion. An array of lasers is used to cool the ion to its quantum ground state, where the momentum and position uncertainties of the ion are at their minimum. The trap is a three-dimensional bowl-shaped region created by the combination of two electric potentials; the ion sits at the bottom of this "harmonic" potential. Switching off one of the potentials creates conditions similar to what is required by the theoretical proposal: a barrier on one side and a sloping electric potential on the other side. The ion moves down that slope, accelerates and gains velocity. “You can have a detector outside the trap and measure the arrival time,” Schmidt-Kaler says. “That is what made it so attractive.”

For now his group has done experiments in which the researchers eject the ion out of its trap and detect it outside. They showed that the time of flight is dependent on a particle’s initial wave function. The results were published in 2021 in the *New Journal of Physics*. Schmidt-Kaler and his colleagues have also performed not yet published tests of the ion exiting the trap only to be reflected back in by an “electric mirror” and recaptured–a process the setup achieves with 98 percent efficiency, he says. “We are underway,” Schmidt-Kaler says. “Of course, it is not tuned to optimize this measurement of the time-of-flight distribution, but it could be.”

That is easier said than done. The detector outside the ion trap will likely be a sheet of laser light, and the team will have to measure the ion’s interaction with the light sheet to nanosecond precision. The experimentalists will also need to switch off one half of the harmonic potential with similar temporal precision–another serious challenge. These and other pitfalls abound on the path between theoretical prediction and experimental realization.

Still, Schmidt-Kaler is excited about the prospect of using time-of-flight measurements to test the foundations of quantum mechanics. “This has the attraction of being completely different from other [kinds of] tests. It really is something new,” he says. “This will go through many iterations. We will see the first results, I hope, in the next year. That’s my clear expectation.” Meanwhile Aristarhov and Das are reaching out to others, too. “We really hope that the experimentalists around the world notice our work,” Aristarhov says. “We will join forces to do the experiments.”

In a yet to be published paper co-authored by Dürr before he died, the closing words could almost be an epitaph: “It should be clear by now that the chapter on time measurements in quantum physics can only be written if genuine quantum-mechanical time-of-flight data become available." Which theory will the experimental data pick out as correct–if any? As Dürr wrote, "It's a very exciting question."

About the Author

Anil Ananthaswamy is author of The Edge of Physics, The Man Who Wasn't There *and* Through Two Doors at Once: The Elegant Experiment That Captures the Enigma of Our Quantum Reality.

Could Gravity's Quantum Origins Explain Dark Energy?

By Conor Purcell

For decades cosmologists have wondered about the nature of dark energy, the proposed antigravitational force behind the accelerating expansion of the universe. Since the 1990s astronomers have observed that the universe is not only expanding, but also increasing its expansion rate. This is very strange, because the collective gravitational pull of all the "stuff" in the universe would be expected to eventually reverse cosmic expansion, or at least slow it down. Instead, just like a ball gently tossed overhead suddenly soaring off into the heavens, some mysterious force–the aforementioned "dark energy"–is pushing far-distant, galaxy-filled regions of space away from us at ever-greater speeds. No known physics has fully explained this phenomenon; it remains a cosmic enigma, and its true, as-yet-unknown nature will profoundly shape the ultimate fate of our universe.

Now, however, a new theoretical study, published in the *Journal for Cosmology and Astroparticle Physics*, suggests dark energy's apparent antigravitational properties may be the natural, inevitable consequence of how gravity works in the first place, at the universe's most fundamental quantum scales. If eventually verified by further cosmological evidence, the idea would represent a major breakthrough in the long quest to mend the schism between physicists' two most cherished theories: quantum mechanics, which describes the microscopic world of particles and fields, and general relativity, which describes the macroscopic cosmos of planets, stars and galaxies. General relativity posits that gravity is an emergent property of curves and warps in space-time–the fabric of reality itself–but the theory loses its predictive power at quantum scales; conversely, quantum mechanics accurately incorporates all other known fundamental forces save for gravity, which fails to fit into the theory. Thus, many physicists suspect a quantum theory of gravity is the only way to unify these two opposing approaches..

According to Daniele Oriti, a co-author of the new paper, the core idea behind any theory of quantum gravity is that gravitation arises from a myriad of tiny, discrete, quantum objects that form a sort of hidden underworld, a deeper substructure beneath the familiar dimensions of space and time. "These quantum objects, which are very difficult to imagine," Oriti says, "are essentially the building blocks of space itself. They do not exist in space, but are themselves the very stuff out of which space is made. If they exist at all, they are absolutely tiny in their size, and are at a microscopic scale which even the most powerful microscopes cannot see."

In the study Oriti and his co-author Xiankai Pang, both at the University of Munich in Germany, focused first on developing a new quantum gravity model by trying to better understand the force's properties at the microscopic level. "Once having constructed our new model," Oriti says, "we decided to track it through time from the beginning of our modeled universe, to see what would happen during the evolution of its expansion. We were definitely surprised when we saw something closely resembling dark energy. The model produced an acceleration of the expansion of the universe at the stage corresponding to the time we are at today, which matches very closely with current observational evidence."

"This is quite an elegant result," says Abhay Ashtekar, an eminent theorist at Penn State who works on modern theories of quantum gravity and who was not involved in the new study. "Because the new approach begins with a general framework for quantum gravity at the subspace level, and then applies it to the cosmological scale, while in other methods one restricts oneself to the cosmological context right from start, the new idea is beginning from a more fundamental perspective than we have done before, and that is an advantage."

Oriti explains that the model's acceleration of the expansion of the universe, during the stage corresponding to today, is caused by interactions between the subspace quantum objects that make up gravity in the theory. After the expanding universe reaches a critical volume, these quantum objects begin to interact with each other in new ways. It is a bit like baking a cake. Imagine a cake where the yeast–in this case the subspace quantum objects–is not so important until a critical temperature–in this case the volume of the universe–is reached, whereafter conditions are just right to kick it into action, causing a rapid expansion. In the quantum gravity model, this is what causes the emergence of the dark energy–like phenomenon, which is characterized by an acceleration of the growth in volume of space.

"In the model, during the early universe, when the volume is small, the quantum objects out of which space emerges, interact in a manner which makes them subdominant compared to their large-scale long-term evolution," says Oriti. "But then, because the universe keeps expanding through time, at some point these interactions become relevant and they start affecting the evolution of the universe–the dynamics of the universe–in a considerable manner, causing an acceleration of the expansion. So, at that stage, the interactions between the quantum objects which make up space produce an acceleration which is similar in description and magnitude to the dark energy cosmologists observe."

"Having a dark energy phenomenological effect like this from a quantum gravity model is very interesting," says Ana Alonso Serrano, a physicist at the Max Planck Institute for Gravitational Physics in Germany, who was also not involved in the study. "I think it is important that we explore our quantum gravity models in this kind of way, so to see if they can make predictions about cosmology and compare them to observations."

"The next step will be to build on their theory, and their model, so to make further predictions which can be compared against real cosmological observations," she says. "But I think there is still a long road ahead before we really establish a good understanding about the quantum nature of gravity, and indeed if there is a firm relationship with dark energy.

About the Author

Conor Purcell is a science journalist who writes on science and its role in society and culture. He has a Ph.D. in Earth science and was the 2019 Journalist in Residence at the Max Planck Institute for Gravitational Physics in Germany.

Escape from a Black Hole

By Steven B. Giddings

Humankind caught its first glimpse of a black hole on April 10, 2019. The Event Horizon Telescope (EHT) team, which uses an Earth- spanning network of radio observatories acting in concert, shared images it had captured of an apparent black hole with 6.5 billion times the mass of our sun in the center of the nearby M87 galaxy. This was a breathtaking achievement–our first view of one of the most mysterious objects in the universe, long predicted but never directly "seen." Even more exciting, the images, and the observations that should follow, are beginning to provide new clues about one of the deepest puzzles in physics.

This enigma is the "paradox" of what happens to information in a black hole. By investigating this question, physicists have discovered that the mere existence of black holes is inconsistent with the quantum-mechanical laws that so far describe everything else in our universe. Resolving this inconsistency may require a conceptual revolution as profound as the overthrow of classical physics by quantum mechanics.

Theorists have explored many ideas, but there has been little direct evidence to help resolve this problem. The first image of a black hole, however, begins to offer actual data to inform our theories. Future EHT observations–especially those that can show how black holes evolve over time–and recent detections of colliding black holes by gravitational-wave observatories could provide important insights and help to usher in a whole new era of physics.

The Information Problem

Though deeply mysterious, black holes seem to be ubiquitous in the cosmos. The EHT observations and the gravitational-wave measurements are just the latest and most robust evidence that black holes, despite sounding fantastical, do indeed appear to be real–and remarkably common. Yet their very existence threatens the present foundations of physics. The basic principles of quantum mechanics are thought to govern all the other laws of nature, but when they are applied to black holes they lead to a contradiction, exposing a flaw in the current form of these laws.

The problem arises from one of the simplest questions we can ask about black holes: What happens to stuff that falls into them? We need a little refinement here to fully explain. First, according to our present quantum-mechanical laws, matter and energy can shift between different forms: particles can, for example, change into different kinds of particles. But the one thing that is sacred and never destroyed is quantum information. If we know the complete quantum description of a system, we should always be able to exactly determine its earlier or later quantum description with no loss of information. So a more precise question is, What happens to quantum information that falls into a black hole?

Our understanding of black holes comes from Albert Einstein's general theory of relativity, which describes gravity as arising from the curvature of space and time; a common visualization of this idea is a heavy ball deforming the surface of a trampoline. This warping of space-time causes the trajectories of massive bodies and light to bend, and we call that gravity. If mass is sufficiently concentrated in a small-enough vicinity, the nearby space-time deformation is so strong that light itself cannot escape a region inside what we call the event horizon: we have a black hole. And if nothing can travel faster than light–including information–everything must get stuck inside this boundary. Black holes become cosmic sinkholes trapping information along with light and matter.

But the story becomes stranger. What may be Stephen Hawking's greatest discovery is his 1974 prediction that black holes evaporate. This finding also led to the startling idea that black holes destroy quantum information. According to quantum mechanics, pairs of "virtual particles" pop into existence all the time, everywhere. Typically such a pair, consisting of a particle and its antimatter counterpart, quickly annihilates itself, but if it forms near the horizon of a black hole, one particle might pop up inside this boundary and the other outside. The outside particle can escape, carrying away energy. The law of energy conservation tells us that the black hole has thus lost energy, so the emission of such particles causes the black hole to shrink over time until it completely disappears. The problem is that the escaping particles, known as Hawking radiation, carry essentially no information about what went into the black hole. Therefore, Hawking's calculations appear to show that quantum information that falls into a black hole is ultimately destroyed—contradicting quantum mechanics.

This revelation initiated a deep crisis in physics. Great advances have followed from previous such crises. For instance, at the beginning of the 20th century, classical physics seemed to predict the inevitable instability of atoms, in obvious contradiction to the existence of stable matter. That problem played a key role in the quantum revolution. Classical physics implied that because orbiting electrons within atoms are constantly changing direction, they continually emit light, causing them to lose energy and spiral into the nucleus. But in 1913 Niels Bohr proposed that electrons actually travel only within quantized orbits and cannot spiral in. This radical idea helped to establish the basis of quantum mechanics, which fundamentally rewrote the laws of nature. Increasingly it seems that the black hole crisis will similarly lead to another paradigm shift in physics.

Quantum Alternatives

When Hawking first predicted black hole evaporation, he suggested that quantum mechanics must be wrong and that information destruction is allowed. Yet physicists soon realized this change would require a drastic breakdown of the law of energy conservation, which would disastrously invalidate our present description of the universe. Apparently the resolution must be sought elsewhere.

Another early idea was that black holes do not completely evaporate but instead stop shrinking at a tiny size, leaving behind microscopic remnants containing the original information. But, scientists realized, if this were true, basic properties of quantum physics would predict catastrophic instabilities causing ordinary matter to explode into such remnants, also contradicting everyday experience.

Obviously something is very wrong. It is tempting to conclude that the flaw is in Hawking's original analysis and that somehow information does escape a black hole emitting Hawking radiation. The challenge here is that this scenario would conflict with a foundational concept of present-day physics, the principle of locality, which states that information cannot move from one place to another superluminally–that is, faster than the speed of light. But according to our definition of black holes, the *only* way to escape one is to travel faster than light, so if information does escape, it must be doing so superluminally, in conflict with locality. In the four decades since Hawking's discovery, physicists have tried to find a loophole to this argument that stays within conventional physics, but none has emerged.

The closest attempt was a 2016 proposal by Hawking, Malcolm Perry and Andrew Strominger, who suggested that a mistake in the original analysis implies information never fully enters a black hole and instead leaves a kind of imprint in the form of what they called "soft hair" outside it. Closer examination seems to be closing this loophole, however, and most experts do not believe this can be the answer. In short, more radical steps appear to be needed.

An obvious idea is that there is some unknown physics that prevents true black holes from existing at all. The conventional picture of black hole formation says that when very large stars burn out and die, their mass collapses under the force of gravity into a black hole. But what if they never reach that stage and actually transform into objects with "better" behavior? In fact, we know that when lower-mass stars such as our sun burn out and collapse, they do not form black holes and instead form dense remnants–for example, white dwarfs or neutron stars. Perhaps some unknown laws of physics also prevent larger stars from forming black holes and instead lead them to become a kind of "massive remnant"–something more like a neutron star than a black hole.

The problem with this suggestion is that we cannot explain what would stabilize such objects–no known physics should prevent their continued collapse under gravity, and any imagined physics that did would apparently require superluminal signaling from one side of the collapsing matter to the other. In fact, conventional large black holes can form from *very* low-density matter. To illustrate, if the 6.5-billion-solar-mass black hole in M87 arose from the collapse of a dust cloud (which is theoretically possible, although the actual process was apparently more complex), it would have happened when the dust reached the density of air at the top of Mount Everest. (Air on top of Everest does not form a black hole because there is not enough of it; one would require an accumulated 6.5 billion solar masses.) Some drastic and superluminal new physical process would need to take over in such a low-density regime to instantly convert the collapsing cloud into a massive remnant instead of allowing a black hole to form.

A related idea is that something could cause black holes to change into massive remnants containing the original information after they form but long before they evaporate. But once again, this story requires nonlocal transfer of information from the interior of the initial black hole to the final remnant.

Despite their problems, physicists have explored versions of both these scenarios. For example, in 2003 Samir Mathur put forward a proposal based on string theory, which posits that fundamental particles are tiny strings. His idea is that a black hole transforms into a "fuzzball," a kind of massive remnant, or that a fuzzball forms instead of a black hole in the first place. Thanks to the complicated physics of string theory and its allowance for more than the traditional four dimensions of space-time, fuzzballs might have a complex higher-dimensional geometry; instead of the sharp traditional boundary of a black hole at the event horizon, a fuzzball would have a fuzzier and larger boundary where one encounters strings and higher-dimensional geometry.

Alternatively a more recent version of a remnant scenario is the proposal that instead of a black hole with an event horizon, a massive remnant forms with a surface "firewall" of high-energy particles where the horizon would be. This firewall would incinerate anything that encountered it, turning it into pure energy that added to the firewall. Both the firewall and the fuzzball, though, share the problem of needing locality violation, and the resulting objects would have other properties that are very hard to explain.

Modifying Locality

A common thread in massive-remnant proposals is that saving quantum mechanics appears to require violation of the locality principle. But doing so carelessly is expected to be as disastrous as modifying quantum mechanics and, in fact, typically leads to another paradox. Specifically, the laws of relativity say that if you send a faster-than-light signal in empty, flat space, observers traveling past you at a high-enough speed will see the signal going backward in time. The paradox arises because this superluminal signaling then allows you to send a message into your past, for example, asking someone to kill your grandmother before your mother is born.

Even though this kind of answer appears to contradict fundamental physical principles, it is worth a closer look. Modifying locality seems crazy, but we have not found an alternative that does not. The severe nature of the black hole crisis strongly suggests a resolution via some subtle violation of the locality principle, one that does not produce such paradoxes. Put differently, quantum mechanics implies information is never destroyed, so information that falls into a black hole must ultimately escape, possibly through some new, subtle "delocalization" of information that might become clear when we can finally find a way to unify quantum mechanics and gravity–one of the most profound problems of present-day physics. In fact, we have other reasons to think such a subtlety could be present. The very idea of localized information–that it can exist in one place and not in another–is more delicate in theories that include gravity than in those that do not, because gravitational fields extend to infinity, complicating the concept of localization.

If information does escape black holes, it might not require a change as obvious and abrupt as the formation of a massive remnant, whether fuzzball, firewall or another variant. The growing evidence for black holes suggests there are objects in the universe that look and act a lot like classical black holes, without large departures from Einstein's predictions. Is Einstein's general relativity so drastically wrong in its description of black holes, or might there be some more innocuous, currently unknown effects that delocalize information and allow it to leak from black holes, avoiding such a dramatic failure of the entire space-time picture?

In my theoretical work, I have found two versions of such effects. In one, the geometry of space-time near a black hole is altered, making it bend and ripple in a way that depends on the information in the black hole–but gently, so that it does not, for example, destroy an astronaut falling through the region where the horizon would ordinarily be found. In this "strong, nonviolent" scenario, such shimmering of space-time can transfer the information out. Interestingly, I have also found that there is a subtler, intrinsically quantum way for information to escape the black hole. In this "weak, nonviolent" scenario, even tiny quantum fluctuations of the space-time geometry near the black hole can transfer information to particles emanating from the hole. The fact that the information transfer is still large enough to save quantum mechanics is related to the huge amount of possible information a black hole can contain. In either picture, a black hole effectively has a "quantum halo" surrounding it, where interactions pass information back to its surroundings.

Notably, these scenarios, despite appearing to require superluminal travel of information, do not necessarily produce a grandmother paradox. The information signaling here is tied to the existence of the black hole, which has a space-time geometry that is different from that of flat space, so that the earlier argument about communicating with the past no longer holds. These possibilities are tantalizing from another perspective: the locality principle is also what prohibits our own faster-than-light travel; the quantum mechanics of black holes seems to be telling us there is something wrong with the present formulation of this principle.

Rewriting the Laws of Physics

So far such a quantum-halo scenario has not been predicted by a more complete theory of physics that reconciles quantum mechanics with gravity, but it is strongly indicated by the need to resolve the problem and by assumptions based on what we see. If such a scenario is correct, it probably represents an approximate description of a deeper reality. Our very notions of space and time, which underlie the rest of science, appear to require significant revision. The present work to understand black holes may be akin to the first attempts to model the physics of the atom by Bohr and others. Those early atomic descriptions were also approximate and only later led to the profound theoretical structure of quantum mechanics. Although modifying locality seems impossible, we might find solace by noting that the laws of quantum mechanics also seemed quite impossible to the classical physicists grappling with their discovery.

Given the immense challenge in sorting out the story of quantum black holes and the more complete theory describing them, physicists are eager for experimental and observational evidence to help guide us. The exciting recent advances have given humankind two direct observational windows on black hole behavior. In addition to the EHT's images of black holes, the Laser Interferometer Gravitational-wave Observatory (LIGO) and its companion facilities have begun to detect gravitational waves from collisions between apparent black holes. These waves carry valuable information with them about the properties and behavior of the objects that created them.

From a naive viewpoint, it seems preposterous that the EHT or LIGO could detect any departure from Einstein's description of black holes. Traditionally his theory has been expected to need modification only when space-time curvatures become extremely large, near the center of a black hole; in contrast, curvatures are very weak near the horizon of a large black hole. But the information crisis I have described suggests otherwise. A large part of the theoretical community has now reached the consensus that some changes to the current laws of physics are needed to describe phenomena not just deep inside a black hole but all the way out past the horizon. We appear to have crossed the Rubicon. For the case of the black hole in M87, the distance at which we expect to find deviations from classical predictions is several times the size of our solar system.

Already LIGO and the EHT have ruled out wilder possibilities that could be considered in an attempt to give a logically consistent description of black holes. Specifically, if black holes were replaced by massive remnants more than about twice the diameter of the supposed black hole, we would have seen signs in the data from both experiments. In the case of the EHT, much of the light that produced the now famous image comes from a region around one and a half times the diameter of the event horizon. And for LIGO, part of the gravitational-wave signal that we detect is likewise produced from the region where the colliding objects reach similarly small separations. Although study of these signals is still in early phases, the EHT and LIGO have revealed very dark and very compact objects that produce signals just like those predicted for unmodified black holes.

Still, it is important to investigate these signals more closely. Sufficiently careful analysis might in fact uncover more clues about the quantum physics of black holes. Even if no new effects are observed, we then have information that constrains possible descriptions of their quantum behavior.

Sufficiently large-diameter remnants are now ruled out, but what about remnant scenarios that modify the black hole description only very near the horizon? Although a complete discussion would require a fuller theory of these remnants–such as fuzzballs or firewalls–we have some initial indicators. Specifically, if these objects had radii barely larger than the radius of the corresponding black hole horizon, then it is likely that neither EHT nor LIGO observations would be able to reveal such a structure because very little light or gravitational radiation escapes from the region very near the horizon.

One possible exception is the possibility of gravitational "echoes." As first suggested in 2016 by Vitor Cardoso of the University of Lisbon, Edgardo Franzin of the International School for Advanced Studies in Italy and Paolo Pani of Sapienza University of Rome, if two such remnants combine to form a final remnant that has similar properties, gravitational waves can reflect off the merged remnant's surface and might be observed. Whereas most near-horizon scenarios are hard to rule out through observation, however, it is difficult to explain how such structures could be stable, instead of collapsing under their own weight to form black holes. Of course, this is a general problem for all massive-remnant scenarios, but it becomes even more challenging in the presence of the extreme forces in such a collision.

Prospects are better for testing some of the scenarios where new interactions behave like subtle modifications of space-time geometry but extend well outside the horizon. For example, in the strong, nonviolent scenario, the rippling of a black hole's quantum halo can distort light passing near the black hole. If this scenario is correct, the shimmering could cause distortions of the EHT's images that change with time.

In my work with EHT scientist Dimitrios Psaltis, we found these changes could happen over roughly an hour for the black hole in the center of our galaxy. Because the EHT combines multihour observations into an average, such effects may be hard to see. But the relevant fluctuation time for the black hole in M87, which is more than 1,000 times larger, is more like tens of days. This work suggests we should look for these distortions by using longer-duration EHT observations than the project's initial seven-day span. If the experiment found such distortions, they would be a spectacular clue to the quantum physics of black holes. If they do not appear, that will begin to point to the subtler weak quantum scenario or to something even more exotic.

The weak, nonviolent scenario is harder to test because of the relative smallness of the expected changes to the geometry. Yet preliminary investigation shows that this scenario can alter how gravitational waves are absorbed or reflected, possibly yielding an observable modification to gravitational-wave signals.

If either scenario is correct, we will learn more not only about what quantum black holes are but also about the deeper laws of nature. Right now we do not fully understand how to think about information localization when gravitational fields are present. Quantum physics suggests that space-time itself is not a fundamental part of physics but instead arises only as an approximation of a more basic mathematical structure. Evidence for quantum black hole effects could help make this concept more concrete.

To learn more, it is important to extend and improve both EHT and gravitational-wave measurements. For the EHT, it would be useful to have significantly longer-duration observations, as well as images of other targets such as our galaxy's central black hole, both of which are anticipated. For gravitational waves, more observations with increased sensitivity would be helpful and will be assisted when additional detectors come online in Japan and India, adding to the existing facilities in the U.S. and Europe. Furthermore, a strong complementary theoretical effort is needed to refine scenarios, to better clarify their origins and explanations, and to assess more thoroughly the question of how significantly they can affect EHT or gravitational-wave signals.

Whatever the resolution to the crisis, black holes contain crucial clues to the basic quantum physics of gravity, as well as to the very nature of space and time. Just as with the atom and quantum mechanics, a better understanding of black holes is likely to help guide the next conceptual revolution in physics. EHT and gravitational-wave observations have the potential to provide us with key information, either by ruling out quantum black hole scenarios or by discovering new phenomena associated with them.

About the Author

Steven B. Giddings is a quantum physicist at the University of California, Santa Barbara, who focuses on high-energy theory, quantum aspects of gravity, and quantum black holes.

The Cosmological Constant Is Physics' Most Embarrassing Problem

By Clara Moskowitz

In every bit of nothing, there is something. If you zoom in on empty space and take out all the planets and stars and galaxies, you might expect a pure vacuum, but you'd be wrong. Instead you would find a dynamic scene, with particles sparking to life and disappearing almost immediately.

Quantum mechanics, the theory governing the infinitesimal world, doesn't allow for nothingness. At any given moment in time and space, energy can never be perfectly zero–there is always some wiggle room. Out of that wiggle room, "virtual" particles can arise–specifically, a pair made of a particle and its antiparticle, which annihilate each other and are gone as quickly as they came. As bizarre as this may seem, experiments have observed the real-world effects of virtual particles. When particle accelerators first measured the mass of the Z boson, it was slightly off from its pure mass because it was sometimes turning into a virtual top quark–one of many observations proving that virtual particles exist.

The effect of all these particles wiggling into and out of being is a thrumming "vacuum energy" that fills the cosmos and pushes outward on space itself. This activity is the most likely explanation for dark energy–the reason the universe, rather than staying static or even expanding at a steady rate, is accelerating outward faster and faster every moment.

The problem with vacuum energy is that there's not enough of it. When scientists first started thinking about the concept, they calculated that this energy should be huge–it should have expanded the universe so forcefully and quickly that no stars and galaxies ever formed. Because that is clearly not the case, the vacuum energy in the universe must be very small–about 120 orders of magnitude smaller than what quantum theory predicts. That's like saying that something weighing five pounds should really weigh five-with-120-extra-zeros-after-it pounds. The discrepancy has prompted some scientists to call vacuum energy "the worst theoretical prediction in the history of physics."

Vacuum energy is thought to be the main ingredient in the "cosmological constant," a mathematical term in the equations of general relativity. The enormous discrepancy between the predicted amount of vacuum energy and the measured amount is often called the cosmological constant problem. "It's generally regarded as one of the most awkward, embarrassing, difficult problems in theoretical physics today," says Antonio Padilla, a physicist at the University of Nottingham in England, who has spent 15 years trying to figure it out. "It suggests there's something missing in our story. I find it exciting–why would you not want to work on that?"

The riddle has enticed some of the greatest minds in physics and elicited a plethora of ideas to solve it. In 2020 New York University physicist Gregory Gabadadze spent an hour summarizing all the concepts theorists have come up with so far in a talk at the Brown University physics department. At the end, one of the audience members asked him which of the ideas he favored. "None of them," Gabadadze replied. They are all too "radical," he said, and all require "giving up sacred principles."

But some physicists say new theoretical work is injecting excitement into the quandary. And recent advances in precision laboratory experiments that probe gravity, as well as the advent of gravitational-wave astronomy, offer hope that some of the proposed solutions to the problem could finally be put to the experimental test–or, at the very least, ruled out.

The Birth of a Problem

The cosmological constant has a checkered history. "It was what you could call a nonsolution to a nonproblem," says physicist Rafael Sorkin of the Perimeter Institute for Theoretical Physics in Ontario. Albert Einstein first invented it in 1917 as a mathematical kludge to force his general relativity field equations to predict a static universe, as he and most scientists then believed the cosmos to be. But in 1929 astronomer Edwin Hubble measured the speeds of many galaxies and found, to his surprise, that they are all moving away from us–in fact, the farther away the galaxy, the faster it was going. His measurements showed that space is expanding everywhere, and no matter where you look, it will seem as if all galaxies are receding because the distance between everything is constantly growing. Faced with this news, Einstein decided a couple of years later to remove the cosmological constant from his equations, calling it "my biggest blunder," according to physicist George Gamow.

For a while the cosmological constant was a footnote of history, but it was quietly preparing for a comeback. In the late 1990s two teams of astronomers were competing to measure how much the expansion of the universe was slowing down as a result of gravity pulling matter inward. In 1998 and 1999 they published their results, based on measurements of special supernovae whose distances could be determined very accurately. The most distant of these supernovae turned out to be much dimmer, and therefore farther away, than expected. The expansion wasn't slowing down at all–it was speeding up. This alarming discovery won three of the teams' leaders a Nobel Prize and prompted cosmologist Michael Turner to coin the term "dark energy" for the mysterious force causing the acceleration. Immediately physicists suggested that the source of dark energy might be the cosmological constant–in other words, vacuum energy. "Perhaps there was more insight in Einstein's blunder than in the best efforts of ordinary mortals," Saul Perlmutter, one of the discoverers of the acceleration, later wrote.

Although the cosmological constant allowed scientists to balance the Einstein field equations again, making them predict an accelerating universe like the one astronomers had observed, the value of the constant didn't make sense. It actually worsened a problem that had been bothering scientists for a while. In the years that the constant lay on the cutting-room floor, physicists had linked this term from general relativity with the concept of vacuum energy from quantum mechanics. But the vacuum energy was supposed to be huge.

One of the first people to notice something was amiss was physicist Wolfgang Pauli, who found in the 1920s that this energy should be so strong that the cosmos should have expanded long past the point where light could traverse the distance between any of the objects in it. The whole of the observable universe, Pauli calculated, "would not even reach to the moon." He was reportedly amused by his estimation, and no one took it seriously at the time. The first to formally calculate the value of the cosmological constant based on quantum theory's predictions for the vacuum energy was physicist Yakov Zel'dovich, who found in 1967 that the energy should make the cosmological constant gigantic. But at the time, scientists thought the universe was expanding at a steady or slowing rate, and most believed the cosmological constant to be zero. The cosmological constant problem was born.

Thirty years later, when astronomers realized that the expansion of the cosmos was accelerating, the problem didn't go away. The amount of acceleration, though shocking at the time, was still minuscule compared with what quantum theory said it should be. In a way, reviving the cosmological constant made the predicament worse. It was one thing to try to imagine why the constant might come out to precisely zero. It became more difficult to understand why it might be just slightly more than nothing. "Its value is very weird," says theoretical physicist Katherine Freese of the University of Texas at Austin. "Even weirder than zero."

Not everyone agrees that this is a problem in need of fixing. The cosmological constant is technically just a constant of nature, a number in an equation that can take on any value, says Sabine Hossenfelder, a theoretical physicist at the Frankfurt Institute for Advanced Studies in Germany. The fact that it has the value it has is just a numerical coincidence. "You could just take the constant and be done with it," Hossenfelder says. "All these debates about why does it have the value it has are not scientifically good questions," she says. Nothing about quantum field theory was falsified when its prediction didn't match astronomical measurements, and the theory is still as useful as it ever was. "I think most people in the cosmology and astrophysics community believe it's a problem because they've been told that for a long time."

Yet many physicists cannot let it go. The unexpected smallness of the cosmological constant is a thread that needs pulling. "It bothers me a lot," Gabadadze says, "and I want some answers."

Theories Galore

Despite the zeal many physicists have for attacking the question, the pace of progress has been frustratingly slow. "It's been more than 50 years since Zel'dovich really pointed out what the problem was, and there's certainly no established, accepted explanation," Padilla says. "Ideas come and go, but generally very little sticks."

Most proposed solutions to the cosmological constant problem fall into three categories: change the general relativity equations that describe the expansion of the universe, modify the quantum field theory equations that predict the amount of vacuum energy, or throw something entirely new into the mix.

Tweaking general relativity could change the mathematical role the cosmological constant plays—or cut it out altogether. Freese and her colleagues, for instance, sought to eliminate the need for the constant to explain the acceleration of the universe by altering the way general relativity calculations should be applied to the expanding cosmos. "Matter and photons might be enough, without adding any new component to the universe, if their role in the equations is different," she says. Her model is based on the idea that extra dimensions, beyond the three of space and one of time that we witness, might be hidden out of sight.

Another angle on updating general relativity is called sequestration, proposed by Padilla and his colleagues. They modify Einstein's theory in a way that seals gravity off so it cannot feel the effects of vacuum energy. "I'm not going to pretend this is the established model," Padilla adds, "but no one's been able to rule it out."

If general relativity isn't the problem, though, maybe quantum mechanics is. Some theorists have suggested that the quantum field theory method of calculating vacuum energy is off. Stefan Hollands of the University of Leipzig in Germany and his colleagues take issue with applying the regular quantum equations to curved space-time, saying they were designed with flat space in mind. If physicists could correctly modify them for curved space, they argue, the cosmological constant problem would go away.

But the resolution might require more than just mathematically finagling the traditional equations. One recent unorthodox idea is a proposal by Steve Carlip of the University of California, Davis, that space-time is fundamentally made of "foam." In this picture, the curvature of space would constantly fluctuate on extremely small scales, well beyond anything we could hope to measure. All this complicated topology would cancel out much of the impact of the cosmological constant, making it very small at the local level. "It's kind of a wild idea," Carlip says. "It is a desperate measure, but so is every other attempt to deal with the cosmological constant, and these are desperate times."

Sorkin, who says Carlip's space-time foam is "going in the right direction," also has his own entry in the field. He works on an approach to unifying quantum mechanics and gravity called causal set theory. According to this model, space-time is fundamentally discrete–meaning that instead of being a smooth, continuous expanse, it is broken up into tiny chunks, individual units of space and time that represent the building blocks of the universe just as atoms are the building blocks of matter. If this is the case, calculating the cosmological constant involves dividing by the number of space-time units in the universe, leading to a value much closer to what astronomers observe.

One of the most prominent–and, by some, most hated–solutions to the cosmological constant problem is called the anthropic principle. This line of thinking agrees that the cosmological constant in our universe has an unlikely value but explains it by saying we live in a multiverse. If ours is just one bubble in a cosmic sea, with different physical laws and constants in each, then there was bound to be one with this value. Most of the others would not lead to a universe with galaxies, stars, planets or life, so the fact that we find ourselves in one of the outliers is only to be expected. Because string theory requires a multiverse, string theorists tend to regard the cosmological constant problem as essentially solved by this reasoning. Other physicists, though, consider this philosophy a cop-out. "It's giving up on the problem," Sorkin says.

All these strategies tend to involve rather dramatic revisions of established physics. "Every single one of them calls for a major revamping of basic principles, either of space-time, say, or the number of dimensions of the universe," Gabadadze says. "They are all distasteful in some way." No single theory has clearly risen above the rest. "At this point it becomes a matter of taste," Carlip says. "Probably the answer is something that nobody's thought of."

Constancy or Quintessence?

The cosmological constant remains the best explanation for dark energy–the mysterious force causing the expansion of space to accelerate. But what if dark energy isn't actually related to the cosmological constant or vacuum energy at all? What if the universe's vacuum energy is somehow perfectly canceled out and the cosmological constant is zero? In that case, dark energy might be the work of something called quintessence.

The notion of quintessence was introduced in 1998 by physicists Robert Caldwell, Paul Steinhardt and Rahul Dave as an alternative explanation for the accelerating expansion of the universe. Quintessence would be some form of energy throughout space with a negative pressure. In contrast to the cosmological constant, quintessence could change over time. One version of quintessence, called phantom energy, postulates an energy whose density increases with the age of the universe, leading to an ultimate "big rip" when space is torn apart by runaway expansion until the distance between particles becomes infinite.

To test whether dark energy is caused by quintessence or the cosmological constant, scientists must determine whether the strength of dark energy has changed over time. Various projects have been gathering data about the expansion rate of space at different cosmic epochs. One example is the Dark Energy Survey, a six-year effort to map galaxies at many distances across a large area of the sky using the Victor M. Blanco Telescope in Chile. The survey's data are in, but scientists are still analyzing them–so far all signs point to dark energy being constant. Another way to find out whether quintessence is real is to look for evidence that this energy has caused the fundamental constants of nature to change over time. No indications of inconstant constants have yet emerged.

Over the next couple of decades experiments should give scientists a better idea of whether the cosmological constant (and the vacuum energy behind it) is the source of dark energy. The Vera C. Rubin Observatory Legacy Survey of Space and Time, planned to begin in 2022 on a telescope currently under construction in Chile, should dramatically improve the precision of current measurements of the history of cosmic expansion. Soon scientists should be able to say much more clearly whether there's room in the data for quintessence or whether an unchanging force has been at work.

Space-time Ripples and Neutron Stars

If, as the evidence seems to show so far, dark energy is truly a result of the cosmological constant, there is still some hope of sorting through the various proposed explanations for its unexpected smallness. Upcoming experiments and astronomical observations may offer a way to discriminate between the proliferation of theories, weeding out some and, just maybe, offering support for others.

Five years ago scientists gained a whole new lens to study the cosmos when they began to detect gravitational waves, the ripples in space-time produced by the collision of huge masses such as black holes and neutron stars. Gravitational-wave observatories such as LIGO (the Laser Interferometer Gravitational-wave Observatory) in the U.S. and Virgo in Europe are now regularly spotting waves produced by cosmic cataclysms, and these waves may prove useful in probing the nature of vacuum energy. Some attempts to solve the cosmological constant problem rely on changes to general relativity that would cause gravity to travel slightly slower than the speed of light. The fact that gravitational waves seem to arrive simultaneously with light from the same events has quashed that idea, ruling out a few theories already. "We had a model 10 years ago called the Fab Four that was aimed at solving the cosmological constant problem," Padilla says. "I'd already started to doubt it, but gravitational-wave data killed it."

Gravitational waves are also revealing strange activity inside neutron stars. These compact remnants of supernovae are so dense that atoms have collapsed, their protons and electrons smashing together to form a mass of almost pure neutrons. This bizarre state gives rise to strange phenomena–for instance, the core of a neutron star might contain a novel phase of matter that would cause a jump in the amount of vacuum energy inside it. Gravitational-wave observatories might be sensitive to the gravitational effects of the extra vacuum energy here, potentially revealing secrets about the nature of vacuum energy.

And while astrophysics experiments search for clues on a cosmic scale, experiments a bit closer to home might also help researchers sort through the cosmological constant hypotheses. Lab setups that probe the universe at the smallest possible distances could be sensitive to some of the alterations of general relativity that physicists are proposing.

An example is the work of the Eöt-Wash group at the University of Washington, where scientists are using an extremely sensitive balance experiment to conduct precision tests of gravity. Their instrument is called a torsion balance: a metal disk with holes cut out of it hangs down from a fine wire, with a similar disk right below it that rotates at a constant rate. The two are separated by distances akin to the width of a piece of paper, and as the bottom disk rotates, its gravitational force causes the upper disk to twist back and forth.

This extremely sensitive experiment allows researchers to track how gravity behaves on scales down to tens of millionths of a meter. If the gravitational force weakens at such close quarters, as some ideas suggest–or if extra, minute dimensions of space are discernible there–the Eöt-Wash team will find them. So far gravity has followed Newton and Einstein's laws to the letter in their tests, and no hidden dimensions have been seen, but the scientists keep adjusting their balance to probe smaller and smaller separations. Even if the group never detects deviations that affect vacuum energy, that won't necessarily be conclusive: it is possible that such changes occur only at distances beyond our reach.

"We'll keep trying," Gabadadze says of attempts to test cosmological constant hypotheses with experiments. "Every generation of physicists since 1960 or so has seen new solutions emerging. Maybe one day some of them will have observational predictions that can be tested, but at this point we're not there." Despite the difficulty of the puzzle, he and other physicists still hope for a solution soon. Perhaps these efforts to understand the cosmological constant problem will reveal deeper truths about quantum physics and general relativity. Or maybe scientists will discover a simpler fix. And even while they're seeking a solution that may never materialize, many physicists revel in the quest.

About the Author

Clara Moskowitz is Scientific American's senior editor covering space and physics. She has a bachelor's degree in astronomy and physics from Wesleyan University and a graduate degree in science journalism from the University of California, Santa Cruz.

Section 3: Quantum Technology

3.1 Basic Quantum Research Will Transform Science and Industry
By Irene Qualters and Antoinette Taylor

3.2 Beyond Quantum Supremacy: The Hunt for Useful Quantum Computers
By Michael Brooks

3.3 Race for the Quantum Internet
By Lee Billings

3.4 "Hybrid" Quantum Networking Demonstrated for First Time
By Dhananjay Khadilkar

3.5 Black Holes, Quantum Entanglement and the No-Go Theorem
By Zoë Holmes and Andrew Sornborger

Basic Quantum Research Will Transform Science and Industry

By Irene Qualters and Antoinette Taylor

The promise of quantum computing seems limitless–faster internet searching, lightning-quick financial data analysis, shorter commutes, better weather prediction, more effective cancer drugs, revolutionary new materials, and more. But we're not there yet. Focusing on narrow benchmarks, such as how many quantum bits, or qubits, the latest computers have (not many), creates a myopic snapshot of a vast technical landscape. The goal goes beyond faster computers to encompass innovations spread broadly across quantum information science, materials, and technologies, such as quantum sensors–a wide field indeed.

Focusing narrowly on computing won't accelerate the arrival of quantum supremacy–the tantalizing promise of a future when quantum computers surpass classical computers in computational tasks of practical importance. That will come only from wide-spectrum research and development spanning fundamental quantum mechanics, information science, materials science, computer science, and computer engineering, among other fields.

The best approach puts science first. Solving basic science problems in quantum science across all its complexities will lay the foundation for an array of future technologies and enable transformative scientific and industrial progress. And make no mistake, those technologies will be major drivers of scientific advancement, the economy, and even national security.

Some day.

To say quantum computing is in its infancy is an overstatement. It's still in the womb. The field is sorting out basic questions about the architectures and technologies for creating and controlling qubits. Qubits are the fundamental processing units of quantum computers, and regardless of the method used to make them, they still don't maintain their "quantumness" long enough to perform tasks much beyond proof-of-concept computations.

The challenge is built into the inherent weirdness of quantum physics itself, which has puzzled the world's most brilliant minds for more than 100 years. Basic questions about how particles behave in the subatomic realm–behavior that enables quantum computing–remain unanswered. The eventual answers will fill in huge blank spots in our understanding of the most fundamental workings of the universe.

That's also what makes quantum science so exciting.

Lacking answers, scientists still debate what makes a quantum computer quantum. Are the conditions of entanglement, superposition, and interference all required? Entanglement is touted as the key ingredient, but that has not been proven. It appears indispensable in some cases, but not in others.

Entanglement occurs when multiple particles can only be described by a global, not an individual, state. This is analogous to reading a book where the individual pages make no sense, but where information emerges once you're read them all. Normal computers struggle mightily to represent entanglement, which severely limits their ability to simulate quantum systems, like pharmaceutical drugs or superconducting materials. This is one reason we need quantum computers.

Superposition stems from the wave-particle duality of elemental particles in the quantum realm, such as electrons, photons, ions, and atoms. Each is a wave function of probabilities regarding its observable state, such as position, spin, polarization (for a photon), or angular momentum. A particle, or qubit, can occupy many states at once. Those states can be "read" much like reading a classical-computing bit as 0 or 1, but a qubit has many more potential values corresponding to the simultaneous probabilities of being 0 or 1. That property speeds up computation.

Decoherence, the nemesis of quantum computing, strikes when environmental factors break down the quantum state. Loosely described as "noise," those factors include entanglement with the external environment or heat. Measuring the value of a qubit also collapses the wave function, and the qubit has to be set up again, like pressing the "clear" button on a calculator.

Because we still do not fully understand how all this works, large-scale quantum computing will remain elusive as science delves deeper into the quantum world. Science is rooted in theory, which must then be observed by experiment, which then refines theory and generates more experiments. As results solidify, practical applications emerge in technology.

In quantum research, for example, we have already seen that scenario emerge in the case of the no-cloning theorem. Formulated by Wojciech Zurek, of Los Alamos National Laboratory, and William Wooters, formerly of Williams College, in the early 1980s the theorem states that an unknown quantum state cannot be exactly copied. In recent years, Los Alamos has developed a quantum-key distribution device based on this principle for creating hack-proof communications, a major step forward in cybersecurity.

That is one example of how basic science research ultimately spawns technology. Zurek continues his theoretical work in quantum mechanics and is currently studying the breakdown of quantum coherence of space time near a black hole. Such pure-science work does not address a technology challenge, but it might someday shed light on why decoherence cripples the particles making qubits in quantum computers.

Closer to home, even today's limited quantum computers are a great place to test theory by simulating quantum physics, since they establish exactly the conditions we wish to study. That capability will advance physics in areas stalled by the limits of classical computing and help answer fundamental physics questions.

So, for example, one project at Los Alamos using a cloud-based, publicly available quantum computer seeks to observe how classical behavior–the reliable determinism we observe in our everyday world–emerges from quantum probabilities. The quantum-classical transition remains one of the great unsolved mysteries in science. It has direct bearing on why quantum computers lose coherence and how we can create durable qubits that maintain coherence long enough for extended calculations, paving the way for large-scale quantum computers.

On another front, research into quantum materials is vital to developing robust quantum computers and a constellation of other technologies. Across the board, the ultimate goal is to create particular, controllable quantum states that we can manipulate. That requires isolating qubits from their environment to prevent unwanted entanglement.

The various architectures being explored for quantum computing depend on different ways of creating qubits. Some computers use the states of super-cold trapped ions, while others use superconducting loops. New research is exploring qubits in defects, or voids, on the surface of solids, such as diamond crystals or atomically thin semiconductors. The work seeks to precisely place these defects where they are needed, offering a path toward controllable quantum states, robust qubits, and circuits of qubits in solid materials at room temperature–a challenging but seemingly attainable goal.

Other research exploits superposition to create quantum "atomtronic" (versus electronic) sensors that precisely detect rotations, acceleration, electromagnetic fields, and the like. The next step is exploiting entanglement. Then a particle needs to hit only one atom of the detector to collapse the superposition and–click! –record a measurement. Related research has "painted" matter-wave guides that work like fiber-optic circuits but are much more sensitive. They could be used to create an "atomtronic" gyroscope, which might one day enable navigation independent of GPS systems.

While theory and basic research march forward and tech giants press ahead exploring the fundamental architecture of quantum computers, the key to extracting their full potential will be algorithms, the set of instructions that tell the computer what to do. They must exploit the unique features of quantum computers without succumbing to the inherent tiger traps of the quantum world. While evidence is highly suggestive, we do not yet know which classes of algorithms may be uniquely enabled by quantum computing.

In work typical of the synergy among quantum theory, quantum information science, and computing, scientists at Los Alamos have adapted algorithms from condensed-matter physics to a new purpose: discovering and developing robust algorithms for the noisy and problematic small-scale quantum computers available today. Related research applies quantum machine learning, an exotic strategy where the quantum computer itself learns to adapt its own algorithms, to perform accurate calculations in spite of its noise.

Quantum computing gets the lion's share of media attention because of the extravagant claims for its potential: it will render current cybersecurity systems obsolete, it will process vast streams of data in the blink of an eye, it will enable artificial intelligence to surpass human intelligence. Some of that might come true, some might not. Only a firm commitment to broad-based quantum research will tell. In any case, that research will lead to unexpected insights, new solutions to old challenges, and surprising benefits to national economic competitiveness, national security, and everyday life.

About the Authors

Irene Qualters is Associate Laboratory Director for Simulation and Computation at Los Alamos National Laboratory.

Antoinette Taylor is Associate Laboratory Director for Physical Sciences at Los Alamos National Laboratory.

Beyond Quantum Supremacy: The Hunt for Useful Quantum Computers

By Michael Brooks

Occasionally Alán Aspuru-Guzik has a movie-star moment, when fans half his age will stop him in the street. "They say, 'Hey, we know who you are,'" he laughs. "Then they tell me that they also have a quantum start-up and would love to talk to me about it." He doesn't mind a bit. "I don't usually have time to talk, but I'm always happy to give them some tips." That affable approach is not uncommon in the quantum-computing community, says Aspuru-Guzik, who is a computer scientist at the University of Toronto and co-founder of Zapata Computing in Cambridge, Mass. Although grand claims have been made about a looming revolution in computing, and private investment has been flowing into quantum technology, it is still early days, and no one is sure whether it is even possible to build a useful quantum computer.

Today's quantum machines have at best a few dozen quantum bits, or qubits, and they are often beset by computation-destroying noise. Researchers are still decades–and many thousands of qubits–away from general-purpose quantum computers, ones that could do long-heralded calculations such as factoring large numbers. A team at Google has reportedly demonstrated a quantum computer that can outperform conventional machines, but such "quantum supremacy" is expected to be extremely limited. For general applications, 30 years is "not an unrealistic timescale," says physicist John Preskill of the California Institute of Technology. Some researchers have raised the possibility that, if quantum computers fail to deliver anything of use soon, a quantum winter will descend: enthusiasm will wane and funding will dry up before researchers get anywhere close to building full-scale machines. "Quantum winter is a real concern," Preskill says. Yet he remains upbeat because the slow progress has forced researchers to adjust their focus and see whether the devices they have already built might be able to do something interesting in the near future.

Judging from a flurry of papers published during the past few years, it's a definite possibility. This is the era of the small, error-prone, or "noisy intermediate-scale quantum" (NISQ), machine, as Preskill has put it. And so far it has turned out to be a much more interesting time than anyone had anticipated. Although the results are still quite preliminary, algorithm designers are finding work for NISQ machines that could have an immediate impact in chemistry, machine learning, materials science and cryptography—offering insights into the creation of chemical catalysts, for example. These innovations are also provoking unexpected progress in conventional computing. All this activity is running alongside efforts to build bigger, more robust quantum systems. Aspuru-Guzik advises people to expect the unexpected. "We're here for the long run," he says. "But there might be some surprises tomorrow."

Fresh Prospects

Quantum computing might feel like a 21st-century idea, but it came to life the same year that IBM released its first personal computer. In a 1981 lecture, physicist Richard Feynman pointed out that the best way to simulate real-world phenomena that have a quantum-mechanical basis, such as chemical reactions or the properties of semiconductors, is with a machine that follows quantum-mechanical rules. Such a computer would make use of entanglement, a phenomenon unique to quantum systems. With entanglement, a particle's properties are affected by what happens to other particles with which it shares intimate quantum connections. These links give chemistry and many branches of materials science a complexity that defies simulation on classical computers. Algorithms designed to run on quantum computers aim to make a virtue of these correlations, performing computational tasks that are impossible on conventional machines.

Yet the same property that gives quantum computers such promise also makes them difficult to operate. Noise in the environment, whether from temperature fluctuations, mechanical vibrations or stray electromagnetic fields, weakens the correlations among qubits, the computational units that encode and process information in the computer. That degrades the reliability of the machines, limits their size and compromises the kinds of computation that they can perform. One potential way to address the issue is to run error-correction routines. Such algorithms, however, require their own qubits–the theoretical minimum is five error-correcting qubits for every qubit devoted to computation–adding a lot of overhead costs and further limiting the size of quantum systems.

Some researchers are focusing on hardware. Microsoft Quantum's multinational team is attempting to use exotic "topological particles" in extremely thin semiconductors to construct qubits that are much more robust than today's quantum systems. But these workarounds are longer-term projects, and many researchers are focusing on what can be done with the noisy small-scale machines that are available now–or will be in the next five to 10 years. Instead of aiming for a universal, error-corrected quantum computer, for example, physicist Jian-Wei Pan and his team at the University of Science and Technology of China in Hefei are pursuing short- and mid-term targets. That includes quantum supremacy and developing quantum-based simulators that can solve meaningful problems in areas such as materials science. "I usually refer to it as 'laying eggs along the way,'" he says.

Bert de Jong of Lawrence Berkeley National Laboratory has his eye on applications in chemistry, such as finding alternatives to the Haber process for the manufacture of ammonia. At the moment, researchers must make approximations to run their simulations on classical machines, but that approach has its limits. "To enable large scientific advances in battery research or any scientific area relying on strong electron correlation," he says, "we cannot use the approximate methods." NISQ systems won't be able to perform full-scale chemistry simulations. But when combined with conventional computers, they might demonstrate an advantage over existing classical simulations. "The classically hard part of the simulation is solved on a quantum processor, while the rest of the work is done on a classical computer," de Jong says.

This kind of hybrid approach is where Aspuru-Guzik earned his fame. In 2014 he and his colleagues devised an algorithm called the variational quantum eigensolver (VQE), which uses conventional machines to optimize guesses. Those guesses might be about the shortest path for a traveling salesperson, the best shape for an aircraft wing or the arrangement of atoms that constitutes the lowest energy state of a particular molecule. Once that best guess has been identified, the quantum machine searches through the nearby options. Its results are fed back to the classical machine, and the process continues until the optimum solution is found. As one of the first ways to use NISQ machines, VQE had an immediate impact, and teams have used it on several quantum computers to find molecular ground states and explore the magnetic properties of materials.

That same year Edward Farhi, then at the Massachusetts Institute of Technology, proposed another heuristic, or best-guess, approach called the quantum approximation optimization algorithm (QAOA). The QAOA, another quantum-classical hybrid, performs what is effectively a game of quantum educated guessing. The only application so far has been fairly obscure—optimizing a process for dividing up graphs—but the approach has already generated some promising spin-offs, says Eric Anschuetz, a graduate student at M.I.T., who has worked at Zapata. One of those, devised by Anschuetz and his colleagues, is an algorithm called variational quantum factoring (VQF), which aims to bring the encryption-breaking, large-number-factoring capabilities of quantum processing to NISQ-era machines.

Until VQF, the only known quantum algorithm for such work was one called Shor's algorithm. That approach offers a fast route to factoring large numbers but is likely to require hundreds of thousands of qubits to go beyond what is possible on classical machines. In a paper published in 2019, Zapata researchers suggest that VQF might be able to outperform Shor's algorithm on smaller systems within a decade. Even so, no one expects VQF to beat a classical machine in that time frame. Others are looking for more general ways to make the most of NISQ hardware. Instead of diverting qubits to correct noise-induced errors, for example, some scientists have devised a way to work with the noise. With "error mitigation," the same routine is run on a noisy processor multiple times. By comparing the results of runs of different lengths, researchers can learn the systematic effect of noise on the computation and estimate what the result would be without noise.

The approach looks particularly promising for chemistry. In March 2019 a team led by physicist Jay Gambetta of IBM's Thomas J. Watson Research Center in Yorktown Heights, N.Y., showed that error mitigation can improve chemistry computations performed on a four-qubit computer. The team used the approach to calculate basic properties of the molecules hydrogen and lithium hydride, such as how their energy states vary with interatomic distance. Although single, noisy runs did not map onto the known solution, the error-mitigated result matched it almost exactly.

Errors might not even be a problem for some applications. Vedran Dunjko, a computer scientist and physicist at the University of Leiden in the Netherlands, notes that the kinds of tasks performed in machine learning, such as labeling images, can cope with noise and approximations. "If you're classifying an image to say whether it is a human face, or a cat, or a dog, there is no clean mathematical description of what these things look like–and nor do we look for one," he says.

Fuzzy Future

Gambetta's team at IBM has also been pursuing quantum machine learning for NISQ systems. In early 2019, while working with researchers at the University of Oxford and at M.I.T., the group reported two quantum machine-learning algorithms that are designed to pick out features in large data sets. It is thought that as quantum systems get bigger, their data-handling capabilities should grow exponentially, ultimately allowing them to handle many more data points than classical systems can. The algorithms provide "a possible path to quantum advantage," the team wrote.

But as with other examples in the machine-learning field, no one has yet managed to demonstrate a quantum advantage. In the era of NISQ computing, there is always a "but." Zapata's factoring algorithm, for instance, might never factor numbers faster than classical machines. No experiments have been done on real hardware yet, and there is no way to definitively, mathematically prove superiority.

Other doubts are arising. Gian Giacomo Guerreschi and Anne Matsuura of Intel Labs in Santa Clara, Calif., performed simulations of Farhi's QAOA algorithms and found that real-world problems with realistically modeled noise do not fare well on machines the size of today's NISQ systems. "Our work adds a word of caution," Guerreschi says. "If order-of-magnitude improvements to the QAOA protocols are not introduced, it will take many hundreds of qubits to outperform what can be done on classical machines." One general problem for NISQ computing, Dunjko points out, comes down to time.

Conventional computers can effectively operate indefinitely. A quantum system can lose its correlations, and thus its computing power, in fractions of a second. As a result, a classical computer does not have to run for very long before it can outstrip the capabilities of today's quantum machines. NISQ research has also created a challenge for itself by focusing attention on the shortcomings of classical algorithms. It turns out that many of those, when investigated, can be improved to the point at which quantum algorithms cannot compete.

In 2016, for instance, researchers developed a quantum algorithm that could draw inferences from large data sets. It is known as a type of recommendation algorithm because of its similarity to the "you might also like" algorithms used online. Theoretical analysis suggested that this scheme was exponentially faster than any known classical algorithm. But in July 2018 computer scientist Ewin Tang, then an undergraduate student at the University of Texas at Austin, formulated a classical algorithm that worked even faster. Tang has since generalized her tactic, taking processes that make quantum algorithms fast and reconfiguring them so that they work on classical computers. This has allowed her to strip the advantage from a few other quantum algorithms, too.

Despite the thrust and parry, researchers say it is a friendly field and one that is improving both classical computing and quantum approaches. “My results have been met with a lot of enthusiasm,” says Tang, who is now a Ph.D. student at the University of Washington. For now, however, researchers must contend with the fact that there is still no proof that today’s quantum machines will yield anything of use. NISQ could simply turn out to be the name for the broad, possibly featureless landscape researchers must traverse before they can build quantum computers capable of outclassing conventional ones in helpful ways.

“Although there were a lot of ideas about what we could do with these near-term devices,” Preskill says, “nobody really knows what they are going to be good for.” De Jong, for one, is okay with the uncertainty. He sees the short-term quantum processor as more of a lab bench–a controlled experimental environment. The noise component of NISQ might even be seen as a benefit because real-world systems, such as potential molecules for use in solar cells, are also affected by their surroundings. “Exploring how a quantum system responds to its environment is crucial to obtain the understanding needed to drive new scientific discovery,” he says.

For his part, Aspuru-Guzik is confident that something significant will happen soon. As a teenager in Mexico, he used to hack phone systems to get free international calls. He says he sees the same adventurous spirit in some of the young quantum researchers he meets–especially now that they can effectively “dial in” and try things out on the small-scale quantum computers and simulators made available by companies such as Google and IBM. This ease of access, he thinks, will be key to working out the practicalities.

"You have to hack the quantum computer," Aspuru-Guzik says. "There is a role for formalism, but there is also a role for imagination, intuition and adventure. Maybe it's not about how many qubits we have; maybe it's about how many hackers we have."

About the Author

Michael Brooks is a freelance writer based in Lewes, England.

Race for the Quantum Internet

By Lee Billings

In a landmark study, a team of Chinese scientists using an experimental satellite tested quantum entanglement over unprecedented distances, beaming entangled pairs of photons to three ground stations across China–each separated by more than 1,200 kilometers. The test verifies a mysterious and long-held tenet of quantum theory and firmly establishes China as the front-runner in a burgeoning "quantum space race" to create a secure, quantum-based global communications network–that is, a potentially unhackable "quantum Internet" that would be of immense geopolitical importance. The findings were published in 2017 in *Science*.

"China has taken the leadership in quantum communication," says Nicolas Gisin, a physicist at the University of Geneva, who was not involved in the study. "This demonstrates that global quantum communication is possible and will be achieved in the near future."

The concept of quantum communications is considered the gold standard for security, in part because any compromising surveillance leaves its imprint on the transmission. Conventional encrypted messages require secret keys to decrypt, but those keys are vulnerable to eavesdropping as they are sent out into the ether. In quantum communications, however, these keys can be encoded in various quantum states of entangled photons–such as their polarization–and these states will be unavoidably altered if a message is intercepted by eavesdroppers. Ground-based quantum communications typically send entangled photon pairs via fiber-optic cables or open air. But collisions with ordinary atoms along the way disrupt the photons' delicate quantum states, limiting transmission distances to a few hundred kilometers. Sophisticated devices called quantum repeaters–equipped with "quantum memory" modules–could in principle be daisy-chained together to receive, store and retransmit the quantum keys across longer distances, but this task is so complex and difficult that such systems remain largely theoretical.

"A quantum repeater has to receive photons from two different places, then store them in quantum memory, then interfere them directly with each other" before sending further signals along a network, says Paul Kwiat, a physicist at the University of Illinois at Urbana-Champaign, who is unaffiliated with the Chinese team. "But in order to do all that, you have to know you've stored them without actually measuring them." The situation, Kwiat says, is a bit like knowing what you have received in the mail without looking in your mailbox or opening the package inside. "You can shake the package–but that's difficult to do if what you're receiving is just photons. You want to make sure you've received them, but you don't want to absorb them. In principle, it's possible–no question–but it's very hard to do."

To form a globe-girdling secure quantum communications network, then, the only available solution is to beam quantum keys through the vacuum of space, then distribute them across tens to hundreds of kilometers using ground-based nodes. Launched into low Earth orbit in 2016 and named after an ancient Chinese philosopher, the 600-kilogram Micius satellite is China's premiere effort to do just that, as part of the nation's $100-million Quantum Experiments at Space Scale (QUESS) program.

Micius carries in its heart an assemblage of crystals and lasers that generates entangled photon pairs, then splits and transmits them on separate beams to ground stations in its line of sight on Earth. For the latest test, the three receiving stations were located in the cities of Delingha and Ürümqi–both on the Tibetan Plateau–as well as in the city of Lijiang in China's far southwest. At 1,203 kilometers, the geographical distance between Delingha and Lijiang was the record-setting stretch over which the entangled photon pairs were transmitted.

For now the system remains mostly a proof of concept because the current reported data-transmission rate between Micius and its receiving stations is too low to sustain practical quantum communications. Of the roughly six million entangled pairs that Micius's crystalline core produced during each second of transmission, only about one pair per second reached the ground-based detectors after the beams weakened as they passed through Earth's atmosphere and each receiving station's light-gathering telescopes. Team leader Jian-Wei Pan—a physicist at the University of Science and Technology of China in Hefei who had pushed and planned for the experiment since 2003—compares the feat with detecting a single photon from a lone match struck by someone standing on the moon. Even so, he says, Micius's transmission of entangled photon pairs is "a trillion times more efficient than using the best telecommunication fibers.... We have done something that was absolutely impossible without the satellite." Soon, Pan says, QUESS will launch more practical quantum communications satellites.

Although Pan and his team later used Micius to distribute quantum keys between ground stations in China and Austria in 2017, enabling secure intercontinental communications, their initial demonstration instead aimed to achieve a simpler task: proving Albert Einstein wrong.

Einstein famously derided as "spooky action at a distance" one of the most bizarre elements of quantum theory—the way that measuring one member of an entangled pair of particles seems to instantaneously change the state of its counterpart, even if that counterpart particle is on the other side of the galaxy. This was abhorrent to Einstein because it suggests information might be transmitted between the particles faster than light, breaking the universal speed limit set by his theory of special relativity. Instead, he and others posited, perhaps the entangled particles somehow shared "hidden variables" that are inaccessible to experiment but would determine the particles' subsequent behavior when measured. In 1964 physicist John Bell devised a way to test Einstein's idea, calculating a limit that physicists could statistically measure for how much hidden variables could possibly correlate with the behavior of entangled particles. If experiments showed this limit to be exceeded, then Einstein's idea of hidden variables would be incorrect.

Ever since the 1970s "Bell tests" by physicists across ever larger swaths of space-time have shown that Einstein was indeed mistaken and that entangled particles do in fact surpass Bell's strict limits. One definitive test occurred in the Netherlands in 2015, when a team at Delft University of Technology closed several potential "loopholes" that had plagued past experiments and offered slim but significant opportunities for the influence of hidden variables to slip through. That test, though, involved separating entangled particles by scarcely more than a kilometer. With Micius's transmission of entangled photons between widely separated ground stations, Pan's team performed a Bell test at distances 1,000 times greater. Just as before, their results confirm that Einstein was wrong. The quantum realm remains a spooky place–although no one yet understands why.

"Of course, no one who accepts quantum mechanics could possibly doubt that entanglement can be created over that distance–or over any distance–but it's still nice to see it made concrete," says Scott Aaronson, a physicist at the University of Texas at Austin. "Nothing we knew suggested this goal was unachievable. The significance of this news is not that it was unexpected or that it overturns anything previously believed but simply that it's a satisfying culmination of years of hard work."

That work largely began in the 1990s, when Pan, leader of the Chinese team, was a graduate student in the laboratory of physicist Anton Zeilinger when he was at the University of Innsbruck in Austria. Zeilinger was Pan's Ph.D. adviser, and they collaborated closely to test and further develop ideas for quantum communication. Pan returned to China to start his own lab in 2001, and Zeilinger started one as well at the Austrian Academy of Sciences in Vienna. For the next seven years they would compete fiercely to break records for transmitting entangled photon pairs across ever wider gaps, and in ever more extreme conditions, in ground-based experiments. All the while each man lobbied his respective nation's space agency to green-light a satellite that could be used to test the technique from space. But Zeilinger's proposals perished in a bureaucratic swamp at the European Space Agency, whereas Pan's were quickly embraced by the China National Space Administration. Ultimately Zeilinger chose to collaborate again with his old pupil rather than compete against him; today the Austrian Academy of Sciences is a crucial partner in the QUESS program.

"I am happy that the Micius works so well," Zeilinger says. "But one has to realize that it is a missed opportunity for Europe and others, too."

For years now other researchers and institutions have been scrambling to catch up, pushing governments for more funding for further experiments on the ground and in space–and many of them see Micius's success as the catalytic event they have been waiting for. "This is a major milestone because if we are ever to have a quantum Internet in the future, we will need to send entanglement over these sorts of long distances," says Thomas Jennewein, a physicist at the University of Waterloo in Ontario, who was not involved with the study. "This research is groundbreaking for all of us in the community–everyone can point to it and say, 'See, it does work!'"

Jennewein and his collaborators are pursuing a space-based approach from the ground up, partnering with the Canadian Space Agency to plan a smaller, simpler satellite that could eventually act as a "universal receiver" and redistribute entangled photons beamed up from ground stations. At the National University of Singapore, an international collaboration led by physicist Alexander Ling has already launched cheap shoebox-size CubeSats to create, study and perhaps even transmit photon pairs that are "correlated"–a situation just shy of full entanglement. And in the U.S., Kwiat is using nasa funding to develop a device that could someday test quantum communications using "hyperentanglement" (the simultaneous entanglement of photon pairs in multiple ways) onboard the International Space Station.

Perhaps most significantly, a team led by Gerd Leuchs and Christoph Marquardt of the Max Planck Institute for the Science of Light in Erlangen, Germany, is developing quantum communications protocols for commercially available laser systems already in space onboard the European Copernicus and SpaceDataHighway satellites.

Using one of these systems, the team successfully encoded and sent simple quantum states to ground stations using photons beamed from a satellite in geostationary orbit, some 38,000 kilometers above Earth. This approach, Marquardt explains, does not rely on entanglement and is very different from that of QUESS–but it could, with minimal upgrades, nonetheless be used to distribute quantum keys for secure communications. Their results appeared in *Optica*.

"Our purpose is really to find a shortcut into making things like quantum-key distribution with satellites economically viable and employable, pretty fast and soon," Marquardt says. "[Engineers] invested 20 years of hard work making these systems, so it's easier to upgrade them than to design everything from scratch.... It is a very good advantage if you can rely on something that is already qualified in space because space qualification is very complicated. It usually takes five to 10 years just to develop that."

Marquardt and others suspect, however, that this field could be much further advanced than has been publicly acknowledged, with developments possibly hidden behind veils of official secrecy in the U.S. and elsewhere. It may be that the era of quantum communication is already upon us. "Some colleague of mine made the joke that 'the silence of the U.S. is very loud,'" Marquardt says. "They had some very good groups concerning free-space satellites and quantum-key distribution at Los Alamos [National Laboratory] and other places, and suddenly they stopped publishing. So we always say there are two reasons that they stopped publishing: either it didn't work, or it worked really well!"

About the Author

Lee Billings is a senior editor for space and physics at Scientific American.

"Hybrid" Quantum Networking Demonstrated for First Time

By Dhananjay Khadilkar

In a world's first, researchers in France and the U.S. have performed a pioneering experiment demonstrating "hybrid" quantum networking. The approach, which unites two distinct methods of encoding information in particles of light called photons, could eventually allow for more capable and robust communications and computing.

Similar to how classical electronics can represent information as digital or analog signals, quantum systems can encode information as either discrete variables (DVs) in particles or continuous variables (CVs) in waves. Researchers have historically used one approach or the other–but not both–in any given system.

"DV and CV encoding have distinct advantages and drawbacks," says Hugues de Riedmatten of the Institute of Photonic Sciences in Barcelona, who was not a part of the research. CV systems encode information in the varying intensity, or phasing, of light waves. They tend to be more efficient than DV approaches but are also more delicate, exhibiting stronger sensitivity to signal losses. Systems using DVs, which transmit information by the counting of photons, are harder to pair with conventional information technologies than CV techniques. They are also less error-prone and more fault-tolerant, however. Combining the two, de Riedmatten says, could offer "the best of both worlds."

Spooky Systems

In quantum networks, information is created, stored and transferred based on the tenets of quantum mechanics. Doing so theoretically allows for levels of security and computational power that surpass anything possible with classical systems.

For instance, classical bits encode information in values of either 0 or 1. Quantum networks can instead use quantum bits, or qubits, which exploit quantum effects to embody 0 and 1 at the same time. To distribute data, such networks also often rely on another effect called quantum entanglement. Famously described by Albert Einstein as "spooky action at a distance," entanglement is generated between particles, such as photons, after they interact closely. Einstein and others considered it "spooky" because, against all intuition, even after being separated over arbitrarily long distances, entangled particles continue to influence each other's behavior. Any change in the state of one of the particles triggers a simultaneous change in the state of the other. Computer scientists long ago realized this effect could enable ultrasecure telecommunications, in which any attempt at eavesdropping would disrupt the entanglement, making the surveillance transparently obvious.

Systems leveraging these quantum effects can take many forms, but they generally follow either a DV or CV architecture. Now scientists at the Kastler Brossel Laboratory in Paris and the U.S. National Institute of Standards and Technology have successfully united both techniques by establishing and distributing entanglement between DV- and CV-encoded states of light within a single quantum network.

Using a complicated assembly of optical components, the team successfully produced photons in two highly entangled states. One of them arose from splitting a single photon between two different paths. The other–a so-called hybrid-entangled state–emerged from entangling a DV optical qubit with a CV qubit, which was held in a superposition of two different phases of light. "By using a special procedure called Bell-state measurement between these two separately entangled states, the entanglement was transferred or 'teleported' to the two systems, [which] never interacted with each other," says Julien Laurat, a professor at Sorbonne University in Paris and senior author of the study. This transference allowed the conversion of the qubits' quantum information from one encoding method to the other, paving the way for incorporating both DV and CV approaches into a single, scalable quantum network.

From Workbench to Workhorse

For Marco Bellini of the National Institute of Optics in Italy, who was not part of the study, what makes it novel and significant is that the researchers successfully swapped entanglement between two light beams carrying two distinct varieties of encoded quantum information. Linking disparate systems together remains a major challenge. But "this experiment has demonstrated what could become an important ingredient of future networks versatile enough to connect memories and processors based on different physical quantum platforms—and faithfully carry a broad range of quantum states, including the DV and CV ones," he says.

Much more work remains to be done before a practical hybrid quantum network is achieved, however, Bellini adds. The current experimental method is extremely inefficient: on average, it generates hybrid entanglement just three times per minute across a distance between a CV qubit and a DV one. "While this rate is still sufficient to accumulate enough data for a proof-of-principle demonstration, it is orders of magnitude too low for any practical application," Bellini concludes.

Further breakthroughs may be imminent. Around the world, other groups are racing to develop and demonstrate additional new quantum-networking protocols—and to close the gap between such preliminary laboratory demonstrations and practical real-world devices.

One such team, led by Bellini, is also working on using the hybrid technique to manipulate entanglement by adding and subtracting single photons to and from classical light fields. Groups in Japan, Russia, Denmark and the Czech Republic are also researching the optical hybrid approach for quantum information. Sooner or later, such hybrid-entanglement experiments should become more compact and efficient, breaking free of the workbench to become workhorses that are compatible with telecoms' existing fiber-optic networks.

About the Author

Dhananjay Khadilkar is a Paris-based journalist who mostly covers science and technology. He also writes on chess.

Black Holes, Quantum Entanglement and the No-Go Theorem

By Zoë Holmes and Andrew Sornborger

Suppose someone–let's call her Alice–has a book of secrets she wants to destroy so she tosses it into a handy black hole. Given that black holes are nature's fastest scramblers, acting like giant garbage shredders, Alice's secrets must be pretty safe, right?

Now suppose her nemesis, Bob, has a quantum computer that's entangled with the black hole. (In entangled quantum systems, actions performed on one particle similarly affect their entangled partners, regardless of distance or even if some disappear into a black hole.)

A famous thought experiment by Patrick Hayden and John Preskill says Bob can observe a few particles of light that leak from the edges of a black hole. Then Bob can run those photons as qubits (the basic processing unit of quantum computing) through the gates of his quantum computer to reveal the particular physics that jumbled Alice's text. From that, he can reconstruct the book.

But not so fast.

Our recent work on quantum machine learning suggests Alice's book might be gone forever, after all.

Quantum Computers to Study Quantum Mechanics

Alice might never have the chance to hide her secrets in a black hole. Still, our new no-go theorem about information scrambling has real-world application to understanding random and chaotic systems in the rapidly expanding fields of quantum machine learning, quantum thermodynamics, and quantum information science.

Richard Feynman, one of the great physicists of the 20th century, launched the field of quantum computing in a 1981 speech, when he proposed developing quantum computers as the natural platform to simulate quantum systems. They are notoriously difficult to study otherwise.

Our team at Los Alamos National Laboratory, along with other collaborators, has focused on studying algorithms for quantum computers and, in particular, machine-learning algorithms–what some like to call artificial intelligence. The research sheds light on what sorts of algorithms will do real work on existing noisy, intermediate-scale quantum computers and on unresolved questions in quantum mechanics at large.

In particular, we have been studying the training of variational quantum algorithms. They set up a problem-solving landscape where the peaks represent the high-energy (undesirable) points of the system, or problem, and the valleys are the low-energy (desirable) values. To find the solution, the algorithm works its way through a mathematical landscape, examining its features one at a time. The answer lies in the deepest valley.

Entanglement Leads to Scramblings

We wondered if we could apply quantum machine learning to understand scrambling. This quantum phenomenon happens when entanglement grows in a system made of many particles or atoms. Think of the initial conditions of this system as a kind of information–Alice's book, for instance. As the entanglement among particles within the quantum system grows, the information spreads widely; this *scrambling* of information is key to understanding quantum chaos, quantum information science, random circuits and a range of other topics.

A black hole is the ultimate scrambler. By exploring it with a variational quantum algorithm on a theoretical quantum computer entangled with the black hole, we could probe the scalability and applicability of quantum machine learning. We could also learn something new about quantum systems generally. Our idea was to use a variational quantum algorithm that would exploit the leaked photons to learn about the dynamics of the black hole. The approach would be an optimization procedure–again, searching through the mathematical landscape to find the lowest point.

If we found it, we would reveal the dynamics inside the black hole. Bob could use that information to crack the scrambler's code and reconstruct Alice's book.

Now here's the rub. The Hayden-Preskill thought experiment assumes Bob can determine the black hole dynamics that are scrambling the information. Instead, we found that the very nature of scrambling prevents Bob from learning those dynamics.

Stalled Out on a Barren Plateau

Here's why: the algorithm stalled out on a barren plateau, which, in machine learning, is as grim as it sounds. During machine-learning training, a barren plateau represents a problem-solving space that is entirely flat as far as the algorithm can see. In this featureless landscape, the algorithm can't find the downward slope; there's no clear path to the energy minimum. The algorithm just spins its wheels, unable to learn anything new. It fails to find the solution.

Our resulting no-go theorem says that any quantum machine-learning strategy will encounter the dreaded barren plateau when applied to an unknown scrambling process.

The good news is, most physical processes are not as complex as black holes, and we often will have prior knowledge of their dynamics, so the no-go theorem doesn't condemn quantum machine learning. We just need to carefully pick the problems we apply it to. And we're not likely to need quantum machine learning to peer inside a black hole to learn about Alice's book–or anything else–anytime soon.

So, Alice can rest assured that her secrets are safe, after all.

About the Authors

Zoë Holmes is the Mark Kac Postdoctoral Fellow at Los Alamos National Laboratory whose research focuses on quantum algorithms.

Andrew Sornborger, a physicist, heads the Quantum Science Center and the Beyond Moore's Law program at Los Alamos National Laboratory.

Section 4: Putting Theory to the Test

4.1 Unexplained Results Intrigue Physicists at World's Largest Particle Collider
By Daniel Garisto

4.2 Elementary Particle's Unexpected Heft Stuns Physicists
By Daniel Garisto

4.3 In a First, Physicists Glimpse a Quantum Ghost
By Karmela Padavic-Callaghan

4.4 New Views of Quantum Jumps Challenge Core Tenets of Physics
By Eleni Petrakou

4.5 The Coolest Physics You've Ever Heard Of
By Karmela Padavic-Callaghan

4.6 Will String Theory Finally Be Put to the Experimental Test?
By Brendan Z. Foster

Unexplained Results Intrigue Physicists at World's Largest Particle Collider

By Daniel Garisto

Editor's Note (10/19/21): On October 19, 2021, LHCb physicists unveiled two more small anomalies that continue a curious pattern of "missing" muons, which collectively hint that these exotic subatomic particles are being produced at lower-than-expected rates. With further validation, these results could become the most promising pathway toward new physics beyond the Standard Model.

If beauty is in the eye of the beholder, then consider a tantalizing new result beguiling the world's particle physicists. Specifically, scientists are interested in fresh data from the LHCb (Large Hadron Collider beauty) detector, an experiment studying the decays of *B*-mesons—particles that contain beauty quarks. During a virtual session of the annual Rencontres de Moriond conference on Tuesday, nearly 1,000 physicists watched as the LHCb collaboration announced evidence for an unexplained discrepancy in the behavior of electrons and their heavier cousins, muons.

Under the Standard Model—the theory that describes elementary particles and the forces they obey, minus gravity—leptons such as electrons and muons are identical except for their mass. So B mesons should decay to a kaon and two muons at the same rate at which they decay to a kaon and two electrons. Yet LHCb is seeing a difference in this rare beauty decay: B mesons seem to decay to muons 15 percent less often than they do to electrons.

"It's certainly intriguing, this new measurement," says Monika Blanke, a theoretical physicist at the Karlsruhe Institute of Technology in Germany, who was not involved with the new research. "If it's eventually confirmed experimentally, then there actually is something beyond the Standard Model that treats the lepton flavors differently."

Physicists have long wondered if muons, electrons and other leptons possess differences besides their mass; the latest LHCb result suggests the answer might be yes. The finding has a statistical significance of 3.1 sigma, which meets the standard baseline for evidence in particle physics. Precisely speaking, 3.1 sigma means that in the absence of new physics, statistical fluctuations would still lead the researchers to see a discrepancy between electrons and muons of *15 percent or more* once every 740 times they performed the experiment. Although this would seem to suggest the observed muon-electron discrepancy is almost certainly more than a mirage, the three-sigma effect, in fact, falls well short of the gold standard of discovery in particle physics: five sigma, which works out to running the experiment 3.4 million times before seeing a statistical fluke that large. (These figures are subtly but importantly different from a one-in-740 or one-in-3.4-million chance of being wrong.)

Why all the fuss about statistics? At LHCb and other experiments, numerous two- and three-sigma discrepancies between electrons and muons have popped up across the years. But so far, none of these results has held up: once more data were collected, the differences between leptons faded away, leaving the Standard Model triumphant.

"If it was only one, I wouldn't be super excited. I've seen other anomalies go away," says Gino Isidori, a theoretical physicist at the University of Zurich, who was not involved with the research. But he is encouraged by the latest LHCb result because it follows a pattern of other measurements that also hint at differences between electrons and muons. For Isidori and other particle physicists, that is reason enough for cautious excitement.

A Thing of Beauty

Located right on the border of France and Switzerland, LHCb is one of many detectors along the Large Hadron Collider's (LHC's) 17-mile loop. Although LHCb also looks at the results from proton-

proton collisions, its focus is on extremely rare decays, such as those of B mesons.

"Rare decays are a different way of trying to find heavy particles," says Patrick Koppenburg, a particle physicist at LHCb. Instead of just smashing protons together and looking for signs of a new particle in the detritus, as the LHC did in its successful brute-force search for the Higgs boson, LHCb looks at minor variations in the one-in-a-million events. That is, a rare decay of a B meson does not directly yield new particles—muons and kaons are old hat—but the rate at which the decay happens can depend on heavy, as-yet-unseen particles influencing the outcome behind the scenes. In the 1960s, for example, rare decays of kaons hinted at the existence of the charm quark before it was directly discovered. LHCb is designed to tease out these needles from the haystack. But even so, the work is difficult and full of experimental uncertainties.

Then there are also theoretical uncertainties to consider: the Standard Model predictions that researchers compare their results against. Part of the excitement surrounding the latest LHCb result is that the specific B meson decay is "clean"—it has a very small theoretical uncertainty. Eliminating one source of error makes it much easier to see if the difference between electrons and muons is genuine.

Since the Standard Model's inception in the 1970s, theoretical physicists have proposed models that explain this difference in the form of a new particle. Two of the top candidates are the Z' (pronounced "zee prime")—a variation on the existing Z boson —and the leptoquark, a particle that would link leptons and quarks. In the coming days and weeks, theoreticians will use the latest result to update their models—and, in fact, three preprint papers were already released within less than 24 hours of the announcement of the LHCb results.

But the physics of this rare decay is far from settled, and much more data are needed before a new particle can be claimed as the culprit. The best option for corroboration will be Belle II, a Japanese experiment. Mikihiko Nakao, a researcher involved in Belle II, expects it will take about five years to catch up to LHCb's sensitivity.

Currently, LHCb is shut down for maintenance. But when it reopens with an upgraded detector next year, it could double all of the data taken over the past decade in just a single year, according to Koppenburg. Upcoming results from Muon g-2, an experiment at the Fermi National Accelerator Laboratory in Batavia, Ill., could also shed light on differences between leptons.

Physicists are aware that this latest result–a bump in the data–is quite possibly just a statistical fluctuation. Having been let down several times before, they are now careful to hedge their bets, trying to avoid conveying certitude or undue hype.

But if it is real–well, that would be beautiful.

About the Author

Daniel Garisto is a freelance science journalist covering advances in physics and other natural sciences. His writing has appeared in Nature News, Science News, Undark, *and elsewhere.*

Elementary Particle's Unexpected Heft Stuns Physicists

By Daniel Garisto

In particle physics, data long outlives the detectors that generate it. A decade ago the 4,100-metric-ton Collider Detector at Fermilab (CDF) reached the end of its life and was shut down, stripped of its parts for use in other experiments. Now a fresh analysis of old CDF data has unearthed a stunning discrepancy in the mass of an elementary particle, the W boson, that could point the way to new, as yet undiscovered particles and interactions.

The W boson is massive, some 80 times heavier than a proton. Crucially, the W boson is responsible for certain forms of radioactive decay, allowing neutrons to convert into protons. Because its mass is constrained by (and itself constrains) many other particles and parameters within the Standard Model—particle physicists' theory of fundamental particles and how they behave—the W boson has become a target for researchers seeking to understand where and how their best theories fail.

Although physicists have long known the W boson's approximate mass, they still do not know it exactly. Plugging data into the Standard Model framework, however, predicts that the so-called W mass should be 80,357 mega-electron-volts (MeV), plus or minus 6 MeV. (One MeV is about twice the mass-energy contained within a single electron.) But in a new analysis published in April 2022 in *Science*, physicists on the CDF collaboration have instead found the W boson mass to be 80,433.5 ± 9.4 MeV. The new measurement, which is more precise than all previous measurements combined, is nearly 77 MeV higher than the Standard Model's prediction. Although these numbers differ by only about one part in 1,000, the uncertainties for each are so minuscule that even this small divergence is of enormous statistical significance—it is exceedingly unlikely to be an illusion produced through sheer chance. The well-studied W boson, it seems, still holds plenty of secrets about the workings of the subatomic world–or at least about how we investigate it. Taken by surprise, particle physicists are only beginning to grapple with the implications.

"Nobody was waiting for this discrepancy," says Martijn Mulders, an experimental physicist at CERN near Geneva, who was not involved with the new research but co-wrote an accompanying commentary in *Science*. "It's very unexpected. You almost feel betrayed because suddenly they're sawing off one of the legs that really support the whole structure of particle physics."

Questing for Quarks

It was a rough measurement of the W boson mass that allowed physicists in 1990 to predict the mass of the top quark with reasonable accuracy five years before that particle was first observed. Then, using the W boson mass and top quark mass, researchers made a similar prediction for the Higgs boson–which bore out spectacularly in 2012. More recently, physicists making such measurements have focused less on refining the Standard Model's core competencies and more on probing its failures–it does not, for instance, incorporate gravity, dark matter, neutrino masses or a number of other troublesome phenomena. Poking at the places where the Standard Model breaks or otherwise deviates from observations, physicists say, is one of the best ways to search for "new physics," their catch-all term for finding additional, possibly more fundamental building blocks of the universe. Until the CDF result, some of the Standard Model's most promising discrepancies included an anomaly investigated at the Muon g-2 experiment at Fermilab and results from the LHCb (Large Hadron Collider beauty) experiment at CERN.

Small anomalies are a dime a dozen, and the vast majority are simply statistical fluctuations arising from the truly enormous numbers of subatomic events produced and recorded by typical particle physics experiments. In such cases, those anomalies fade away as even greater volumes of data are gathered. This latest anomaly appears more promising, though, because there is already so much preexisting high-quality information on the W boson's mass, and the theoretical prediction of the particle's mass has very low uncertainty. And, perhaps most importantly, the CDF collaboration has been extremely careful. The experiment was "blinded" to minimize the risk of human bias, meaning that physicists analyzing its data were kept in the dark about its results until their work was completed. When the CDF's measured value for the W mass was revealed to team members in November 2020, "it was a moment of stunned silence," says the study's corresponding author, Ashutosh Kotwal. "The realization of what that unblinded number meant–that, of course, is pure gold."

Since then, the results have gone through multiple further rounds of peer review–but that only guarantees the physicists have done their homework, not that they have found new physics.

Mining the Data

To measure the mass of a W boson, one must first build a particle collider. The Tevatron, which ran from 1983 to 2011, was a 3.9-mile (6.3-kilometer) loop where protons crashed into antiprotons at up to about two tera-electron-volts (TeV)–some 25 times the mass of a W boson. The CDF experiment, located along the loop, sought signs of W bosons in these collisions from 2002 until the Tevatron shut down.

But one cannot simply observe a W boson; it decays into other particles far too quickly to register in any detector. Instead physicists must infer its presence and properties by studying those decay products–chiefly electrons and muons. Counting carefully, the CDF team found about four million events in the experiment's data attributable to a W boson decay. By measuring the energy deposited in the CDF detector by those events' electrons and muons, the physicists worked backward to figure out how much energy–or mass–the W boson originally had.

This work took a decade because of the numerous uncertainties in the data, Kotwal says. To reach its unprecedented level of precision–twice as precise as the previous best single experiment measurement of the W boson mass, which was made by the ATLAS collaboration—the CDF team quadrupled their dataset and also used new techniques. These included modeling proton and antiproton collisions and conducting a new, more thorough examination of the decommissioned detector's operational quirks–even using old cosmic-ray data to map its layout down to the micron.

That was enough to elevate the researchers' anomalous result to remarkable heights of statistical significance: nearly seven sigma, in the parlance of statistics. Seven sigma means that if no new physics affected the W boson, discrepancies at least as large as the one observed would still arise from pure chance once every 800 billion times the experiment was run. Even in the world of particle physics, where astronomical numbers are the norm, this almost seems like overkill: the field's "gold standard" threshold for statistical significance is only five sigma, which corresponds to a given effect appearing through chance once every 3.5 million runs. Crucially, the seven-sigma value of the CDF team's new measurement does not mean that result has a 99.999999999 percent chance of being new physics. It does not even mean other measurements of the W mass are wrong. Rather a seven-sigma result means that whatever the CDF collaboration is seeing is not by chance. It is a call to further inquiry, not a conclusion.

To determine the anomaly's source, corroboration from other experiments is needed. "It's a very spectacular result," says Guillaume Unal, ATLAS's physics coordinator, who was not involved in the new study. "It's a very complex and challenging measurement, and it's also a very important one to really probe the Standard Model with good accuracy." ATLAS is currently working to improve its measurement of the W mass, and Unal says using data from the LHC's second run, which concluded in 2018, may allow them to get close to CDF's precision.

In the meantime, theorists will pounce on this new result to produce myriad possible explanations. Although the LHC has ruled out many permutations of supersymmetry (SUSY)–a set of theories positing that elementary particles have "superparticle" partners–one culprit that could be shifting the W boson's mass ever so slightly is a cohort of relatively light supersymmetric particles.

"Of course, [the LHC constraints] are becoming more and more stringent," says Manimala Chakraborti, a theoretical physicist at the Nicolaus Copernicus Astronomical Center of the Polish Academy of Sciences, who is not part of the CDF collaboration. "But still, you can find regions of allowed parameter space for SUSY."

At a time when new colliders are being proposed, and the LHC is preparing to launch another campaign of collisions after a massive overhaul, the announcement of a seven-sigma-magnitude anomaly from a long-gone experiment whose detectors have been cannibalized may seem strange.

But the collaboration continues to meet to assess and refine the fruits of the experiment's run. "Detective work itself is what keeps us going," Kotwal says. "The clues are all there.... It's like Sherlock Holmes. The person may be gone, but the footprints are still there."

About the Author

Daniel Garisto is a freelance science journalist covering advances in physics and other natural sciences. His writing has appeared in Nature News, Science News, Undark, *and elsewhere.*

In a First, Physicists Glimpse a Quantum Ghost

By Karmela Padavic-Callaghan

The wave function—an abstract concept used to predict the behavior of quantum particles—is the bedrock on which physicists have built their understanding of quantum mechanics. But this bedrock itself is not something physicists have a perfect grasp of, literally or philosophically. A wave function is not something one can hold in their hand or put under a microscope. And confusingly, some of its properties simply seem not to be real. In fact, mathematicians would openly label them as imaginary: so-called imaginary numbers—which arise from seemingly nonsensical feats such as taking the square roots of negative integers—are an important ingredient of a wave function's well-proved power to forecast the results of real-world experiments. In short, if a wave function can be said to "exist" at all, it does so at the hazy crossroads between metaphysical mathematics and physical reality.

Now researchers at the University of California, Santa Barbara, and their colleagues have made big strides in bridging these two realms: for the first time, they reconstructed a wave function from a measurement of how a semiconductor material responds to an ultrafast pulse of light. Appearing in *Nature* in November 2021, the team's work may help take electronics engineering and quantum materials design into a new era of fine-tuned understanding and precisely controlled innovation.

For real-world applications, such as modern electronics, the somewhat mysterious wave function is physicists' best source of information about what actually happens inside of some new gadget. To predict how fast an electron moves inside a material or how much energy it can carry, they must start their calculations with the so-called Bloch wave function—named for physicist Felix Bloch, who devised it in 1929. This is especially important for engineering quantum devices, says Joe Costello, a physics student at UCSB and co-lead author of the recent study. "If you're thinking about building any sort of device that takes advantage of quantum mechanics, you're going to need to know its [wave function's] parameters really well," he emphasizes.

This includes the wave function's so-called phase, a fully imaginary parameter that is nonetheless often crucial for designing quantum computers. "What has been characterized for a long time is the energies [of the electrons]. That's the basis for all electronics," says Mackillo Kira, a physicist at the University of Michigan, who read an earlier draft of the study but was not directly involved in the work. "But now, with quantum information technology, the next level is to go beyond that and eventually get these [wave function] phases."

To make it to that next level, the team used two lasers and the semiconductor material gallium arsenide. Their experiment consisted of three steps: First, they hit the electrons inside the material with a pulse of near-infrared laser light. This gave those particles extra energy so they would start to quickly race through the semiconductor. When each negatively charged electron started its race, a so-called hole, something like its shadow particle–identical to the electron but positively charged–moved with it. Next, the researchers used another laser pulse to tear the hole and the electron apart, then quickly allowed them to reunite–a sort of quantum version of Peter Pan losing his shadow and having it reattached. When the hole and the electron recombined, the extra energy each accumulated while running solo was released as a burst of light.

Ten years ago a team of physicists led by Mark Sherwin of UCSB noticed something curious about these bursts: their properties were inexplicably sensitive to the properties of the laser pulses that started the particle run in the first place. Sherwin and his colleagues realized that there was significant and largely unexplored nuance to how a semiconductor's electrons react to light. "This was unexpected," he recalls. "But we decided to explore it further and started systematically looking at it." In the new work, calculations done by postdoctoral scholar Qile Wu, a member of Sherwin's team and co-lead author of the study, proved that this telltale sensitivity is more than a mere curiosity because it can be used to reconstruct the Bloch wave functions of holes in a semiconductor.

The connection between the absorbed laser light and the emitted flash revealed itself in measurements of a property called polarization, or the direction in which light waves oscillate as they travel. In the experiment, the polarization of laser light influenced the phases of the wave functions of the running electrons and of their shadowy partners, the holes. When the reunion of the two produced light at the end of the experiment, the polarization of that flash was determined by these two wave function phases. Because such phases are typically represented as imaginary rather than real numbers in physicists' equations, relating them to the very real and measurable polarization of light was a breakthrough for Wu and his collaborators. Shambhu Ghimire, a physicist at Stanford University, who was not involved with the work, underscores exactly this feature of the new study: it used light to obtain information that was previously seen as purely mathematical. "These [light-based] methods can sometimes be difficult or really conceptually challenging, but most of the time, they provide access to this imaginary part of the complex number [wave function] that you do not have access to with other, conventional methods," he says. Further, the team managed to reverse engineer whole Bloch wave functions from those same polarization measurements.

Ghimire further notes that the kind of laser light the UCSB researchers used is important beyond its polarization. They employed ultrafast laser pulses, hitting the electrons with light for as little as a trillionth of a second. Electrons in solids tend to bump into atoms instead of moving uninterrupted, so being able to control them with such celerity was crucial for the team to carry out its Peter-Pan-and-his-shadow manipulation of the electron and the hole. Otherwise, in any given run of the experiment, one or the other would likely slam into some atomic obstacle, preventing reunification. Seamus O'Hara, another co-lead author of the study and a Ph.D. student in Sherwin's group, credits some of that technical advantage to the team's use of UCSB's state-of-the-art Free-Electron Lasers facility.

But the impact of the work will likely extend beyond specialized facilities and simple semiconductors. In gallium arsenide, Wu's theoretical research showed, very few properties of the reemitted light have to be known for a mathematical reconstruction of Bloch wave functions. Other semiconductor materials may require more complete–and perhaps elusive–knowledge, however. "This work is fascinating as a very fundamental demonstration of something you can do where the answer is really well defined," says Mette Gaarde, a physicist at Louisiana State University, who was also not part of the study. "But the implication is that you could potentially use this to learn something about more complex structures."

The UCSB team is already making ambitious plans for next steps. Going forward, the researchers are interested in applying their technique to materials in which electrons strongly interact with one another or where laser light would excite particles more exotic than electrons and holes. "We're looking for new materials. If people have semiconductors that they would like to have looked at, we're excited to try," Costello says, eager for more opportunities to glimpse the intangible world of wave functions many more times.

About the Author

Karmela Padavic-Callaghan is an assistant professor at Bard High School Early College Manhattan, where she teaches calculus and physics.

New Views of Quantum Jumps Challenge Core Tenets of Physics

By Eleni Petrakou

Quantum mechanics, the theory that describes the physics of the universe at very small scales, is notorious for defying common sense. Consider, for instance, the way that standard interpretations of the theory suggest change occurs in the quantum turf: shifts from one state to another supposedly happen unpredictably and instantaneously. Put another way, if events in our familiar world unfolded similarly to those within atoms, we would expect to routinely see batter becoming a fully baked cake without passing through any intermediate steps. Everyday experience, of course, tells us this is not the case, but for the less accessible microscopic realm, the true nature of such "quantum jumps" has been a major unsolved problem in physics.

In recent decades, however, technological advancements have allowed physicists to probe the issue more closely in carefully arranged laboratory settings. The most fundamental breakthrough arguably came in 1986, when researchers for the first time experimentally verified that quantum jumps are actual physical events that can be observed and studied. Ever since, steady technical progress has opened deeper vistas upon the mysterious phenomenon. Notably, an experiment published in 2019 overturned the traditional view of quantum jumps by demonstrating that they move predictably and gradually once they start–and can even be stopped midway.

That experiment, performed at Yale University, used a setup that let the researchers monitor the transitions with minimal intrusion. Each jump took place between two energy values of a superconducting qubit, a tiny circuit built to mimic the properties of atoms. The research team used measurements of "side activity" taking place in the circuit when the system had the lower energy. This is a bit like knowing which show is playing on a television in another room by only listening for certain key words. This indirect probe evaded one of the top concerns in quantum experiments—namely, how to avoid influencing the very system that one is observing. Known as "clicks" (from the sound that old Geiger counters made when detecting radioactivity), these measurements revealed an important property: jumps to the higher energy were always preceded by a halt in the "key words," a pause in the side activity. This eventually permitted the team to predict the jumps' unfolding and even to stop them at will.

Now a new theoretical study delves deeper into what can be said about the jumps and when. And it finds that this seemingly simple and fundamental phenomenon is actually quite complex.

Catch Me if You Can

The study, published in *Physical Review Research*, models the step-by-step, cradle-to-grave evolution of quantum jumps—from the initial lower-energy state of the system, known as the ground state, then a second one where it has higher energy, called the excited state, and finally the transition back to the ground state. This modeling shows that the predictable, "catchable" quantum jumps must have a noncatchable counterpart, says author Kyrylo Snizhko, a postdoctoral researcher now at Karlsruhe Institute of Technology in Germany, who was formerly at the Weizmann Institute of Science in Israel, where the study was performed.

Specifically, by "noncatchable" the researchers mean that the jump back to the ground state will not always be smooth and predictable. Instead the study's results show that such an event's evolution depends on how "connected" the measuring device is to the system (another peculiarity of the quantum realm, which, in this case, relates to the timescale of the measurements, compared with that of the transitions). The connection can be weak, in which case a quantum jump can also be predictable through the pause in clicks from the qubit's side activity, in the way used by the Yale experiment.

The system transitions by passing through a mixture of the excited state and ground state, a quantum phenomenon known as superposition. But sometimes, when the connection exceeds a certain threshold, this superposition will shift toward a specific value of the mixture and tend to stay at that state until it moves to the ground unannounced. In that special case, "this probabilistic quantum jump cannot be predicted and reversed midflight," explains Parveen Kumar, a postdoctoral researcher at the Weizmann Institute and co-author of the most recent study. In other words, even jumps for which timing was initially predictable would be followed by inherently unpredictable ones.

But there is yet more nuance when examining the originally catchable jumps. Snizhko says that even these possess an unpredictable element. A catchable quantum jump will always proceed on a "trajectory" through the superposition of the excited and ground states, but there can be no guarantee that the jump will ever finish. "At each point in the trajectory, there is a probability that the jump continues and a probability that it is projected back to the ground state," Snizhko says. "So the jump may start happening and then abruptly get canceled. The trajectory is totally deterministic—but whether the system will complete the trajectory or not is unpredictable."

This behavior appeared in the Yale experiment's results. The scientists behind that work called such catchable jumps "islands of predictability in a sea of uncertainty." Ricardo Gutiérrez-Jáuregui, a postdoctoral researcher at Columbia University and one of the authors of the corresponding study, notes that "the beauty of that work was to show that in the absence of clicks, the system followed a predetermined path to reach the excited state in a short but nonzero time. The device, however, still has a chance to 'click' as the system transitions through this path, thus interrupting its transition."

"Quantum Physics is Broken!"

Zlatko Minev, a researcher at the IBM Thomas J. Watson Research Center and lead author of the earlier Yale study, notes that the new theoretical paper "derives a very nice, simple model and explanation of the quantum jump phenomenon in the context of a qubit as a function of the parameters of the experiment." Taken together with the experiment at Yale, the results "show that there is more to the story of discreteness, randomness and predictability in quantum mechanics than commonly thought." Specifically, the surprisingly nuanced behavior of quantum jumps–the way a leap from the ground state to the excited state can be foretold–suggests a degree of predictability inherent to the quantum world that has never before been observed. Some would even consider it forbidden, had it not already been validated by experiment. When Minev first discussed the possibility of predictable quantum jumps with others in his group, a colleague responded by shouting back, "If this is true, then quantum physics is broken!"

"In the end, our experiment worked, and from it one can infer that quantum jumps are random and discrete," Minev says. "Yet on a finer timescale, their evolution is coherent and continuous. These two seemingly opposed viewpoints coexist."

As to whether such processes can apply to the material world at large–for instance, to atoms outside a quantum lab–Kumar is undecided, in large part because of how carefully specific the study's conditions were. "It would be interesting to generalize our results," he says. If the results turn out similar for different measurement setups, then this behavior–events that are in some sense both random and predictable, discrete yet continuous–could reflect more general properties of the quantum world.

Meanwhile the predictions of the study could get checked soon. According to Serge Rosenblum, a researcher at the Weizmann Institute who did not participate in either study, these effects can be observed with today's state-of-the-art superconducting quantum systems and are high on the list of experiments for the institute's new qubits lab. "It was quite amazing to me that a deceptively simple system such as a single qubit can still hide such surprises when we measure it," he adds.

For a long time, quantum jumps–the most basic processes underlying everything in nature–were considered nearly impossible to probe. But technological progress is changing that. Kater Murch, an associate professor at Washington University in St. Louis, who did not participate in the two studies, remarks, "I like how the Yale experiment seems to have motivated this theory paper, which is uncovering new aspects of a physics problem that has been studied for decades. In my mind, experiments really help drive the ways that theorists think about things, and this leads to new discoveries."

The mystery might not just be going away, though. As Snizhko says, "I do not think that the quantum jumps problem will be resolved completely any time soon; it is too deeply ingrained in quantum theory. But by playing with different measurements and jumps, we might stumble upon something practically useful."

About the Author

Eleni Petrakou, PhD, is trained in experimental particle physics and has studied and worked at CERN, National Taiwan University, the Greek National Research Center, and, most recently, the Center for Axion and Precision Physics Research (CAPP) in South Korea.

The Coolest Physics You've Ever Heard Of

By Karmela Padavic-Callaghan

When it comes to furthering our overall understanding of the physical world, ultracold quantum gases are awfully promising. As renowned physicist Richard Feynman argued, to fully understand nature, we need quantum means of simulation and computation. Ultracold atomic systems have, in the past 30 years, proven to be amazing quantum simulators. The number of applications for these systems as such simulators is nothing short of overwhelming, ranging from engineering artificial crystals to providing new platforms for quantum computing. In its brief history, ultracold atomic experimental research has enhanced physicists' understanding of a truly vast array of important phenomena.

One of the revelations of quantum mechanics is that any object can be seen as a wave (even you!) when an appropriate experimental test is used. Properties of these so-called matter waves depend on their temperature; at high temperatures they have short wavelengths and look and behave particlelike because all the peaks and valleys are so close together that they cannot be told apart. If we lower temperatures to much less than a single kelvin, the wave nature of matter becomes more pronounced and wavelike behaviors more important. What happens then with a large collection of very cold atoms that behave like a large collection of waves? They can all align and overlap to form a single wave, something that was historically called a macroscopic wave function. Such a system–a condensate in physics parlance–is a fundamentally quantum state of matter.

Quantum condensates were theoretically predicted in the mid-1920s, but it was only in the late 1990s that experimental physicists kicked off a revolution (recognized with two Nobel Prizes) by using lasers and magnets to reach sufficiently low temperatures for the transition to these phases of matter to happen. Light can interact with atoms and thus change their energies. Atoms also experience forces when placed in nonuniform magnetic fields. Physicists used these two properties to trap clouds of atoms such as rubidium and eventually lower their temperature to picokelvins–trillionths of a degree above absolute zero. Remarkably, experiments in which these extremely low temperatures can be reached, and quantum states of matter are engineered, fit in an average-sized room, on a large table with the ultracold atom gas frequently visible to the naked eye. The coldest places in the universe can often be found in a room on your local college campus, and they are likely controlled by a graduate student.

But it's not just making something the coldest or the most quantum that excites physicists; it's that ultracold atoms can be controlled and manipulated very precisely. Theoretical physicists have been especially emboldened by the possibility of engineering a quantum system by moving ultracold atoms around and fine-tuning the way in which they interact. To a theorist, a physical system such as a novel material that has some odd or unexpected property is a frustrating black box that is hard to describe with mathematical equations.

An ultracold atomic experiment can be the exact opposite, bringing equations to life and determining whether they measure up to nature. Many minimal, prototypical models, extensively studied at the level of mathematical equations but not necessarily matched by any naturally found material, can be engineered in ultracold atomic experiments. Since the late 1990s physicists of all sorts have embraced this idea and pushed it in every direction they could imagine.

As one example, adding counterpropagating laser beams to an ultracold atomic sample creates an optical lattice and turns the system into an artificial crystal. Whereas a physical crystal has to be grown carefully, an ultracold artificial crystal can be changed from one shape to another through adjustments to laser beams. Even more advantageously, such artificial crystals are typically very clean, and researchers can add in disorder by using more lasers. This means they can "reverse engineer" some of the effects of disorder. If a crystal is grown and then studied, it can be difficult to determine how much "dirt" in that sample actually matters for experimental outcomes. If researchers can control the disorder, then they can be very precise about determining its consequences.

From the very first ultracold atomic experiments, they have been really important for studying fluids having zero viscosity, or superfluids. When does a normal fluid become a superfluid? Can something similar to sound propagate through a superfluid? What happens if a container of superfluid is rotated? Many such fundamental questions have been answered through simulations with ultracold atoms.

For instance, rotating a superfluid has been predicted to give rise to the appearance of vortices–small hurricanes of quantum fluid–as a consequence of basic properties of the macroscopic wave function. Researchers are learning about quantum turbulence by observing and manipulating these vortices, thinking of them as controllable building blocks of more chaotic superfluid flows. Precise models for turbulent quantum flows have historically eluded theorists, which makes ultracold atomic simulations the first line of attack for this difficult problem.

As with studies of superfluids, many efforts have been made to simulate superconductors. They are perfect conductors having no resistance; no energy is wasted as electric current runs through them. As this is in contrast with all conductors used to supply electricity to businesses and households, it is a very active area of research to try to simulate a superconductor that does not have to be very cold. Whereas a physicist's notion of "very cold" may not quite match the colloquial use of the phrase (a "cold atom" in physics jargon is vastly colder than a cold pint of ice cream in your fridge), even a few kelvins' worth of difference could be meaningful for applications of superconductors outside the lab.

Theoretical physicists have debated various high-temperature superconducting models for years, and ultracold atomic studies have been one of the prime ways to put those, sometimes conflicting, theories to the test. Experimental physicists can also make a superfluid of ultracold atoms become something like a superconductor in a process called BEC-BCS crossover. This crossover has been theorized in semiconductors and neutron stars but never unequivocally confirmed in any system other than ones consisting of extremely cold atoms.

Superconductors and superfluids are both fundamentally quantum phases of matter, making up something like a quantum expansion of the liquid-solid-vapor list of phases you may have learned in school. Ultracold atomic experiments continue to simulate even more novel quantum phases of matter. One striking example from 2019 is simulation of a quantum supersolid. A supersolid, like a superfluid, flows without any friction between the atoms that make it up but also has a periodic, crystal-like structure like solids do. It is a seemingly paradoxical state of matter whose existence was debated for almost 50 years before ultracold atomic experiments provided a definitively affirmative conclusion.

Many so-called topological phases of matter have also been realized in ultracold systems. Some of these experiments simulate, and generalize, the quantum Hall effect, which was first observed in more traditional experiments with semiconductors. Because many topological states of matter have properties unaffected by disorder, they are a very promising setting for quantum computation. In this way, realizing topological models in a very tunable ultracold atomic system means that physicists are able to not only simulate a new phase of matter but also immediately put it to use, getting closer to making a quantum computer.

Even if ultracold atomic systems have not been turned into quantum computation machines just yet, they can often be used to "beat" classical supercomputers in terms of enabling researchers to learn something new about fundamental physics. One example is that of many-body physics. In quantum mechanics, a system that has more than a few interacting particles is almost always a system where it is very difficult to calculate, and therefore predict, anything precisely. And yet real materials consist of millions of atoms!

Ultracold atomic systems have been invaluable for studying highly interacting many-body systems, uncovering phenomena such as systems failing to reach thermal equilibrium and never losing "memory" of their initial state. Physicists often resort to computational methods and supercomputers to study these systems, but a simulation with ultracold atoms can be a more direct way to attack some of their questions. Failure to equilibrate is of great interest in statistical physics, and the advent of ultracold atomic experiments has reinforced it as a very active field of contemporary physics research.

As for me personally, despite being trained in the broader discipline of condensed matter physics, I spent my six years as a graduate student coming back to ultracold atoms over and over again. Mostly I studied superfluid bubbles (hollow shells) made of ultracold atoms. This led me to the work of NASA scientists who launched an ultracold atom experiment into space to explore how it will be affected by extremely low gravity. This experiment is ongoing onboard the International Space Station, and theorists like me who made predictions about what it will find are anxiously awaiting new results.

In a way, it is fitting that studying hollow ultracold shells caused me to think about space, as part of the motivation for this research lies with neutron stars. Physicists don't really know what you would find if you could observe the inside of neutron star, but many theories suggest that it looks like an onion with layers of superconductors and superfluids. Studying superfluid shells in labs could then lead to a better understanding of some of these layers that reside in stars that are so far away that scientists may never be able to study them directly. Moreover, measurements of radio signals coming from neutron stars suggest that superfluid vortices within them may affect their rotation.

Ultracold atomic experiments have excelled in studying exactly those vortices with great precision. I spent several years working on mathematical arguments for what a vortex in a hollow shell of ultracold atoms might do if the whole thing started rotating. I have badgered a fair number of my experimental colleagues with questions about engineering such a system in their labs, and the fact that this is even something we can talk about, some semblance of simulating the quantum innards of a neutron star, still seems to me a little bit like science fiction.

My latest ultracold obsession came when I learned about quasiperiodicity in one-dimensional chains of ultracold atoms. The puzzle hiding behind the jargon is simple: physicists know well how structures of atoms in which they repeat with a regular period behave in nature, but what happens if that period is an irrational number? Such systems are called quasiperiodic, and studying them led cognitive scientist Douglas Hofstadter in 1976 to discover a famous fractal plot later dubbed his butterfly. Hofstadter's plot is self-similar: if you zoom in or zoom out any amount, it still looks the same.

This property implies that physical states having fractional dimensions can exist in nature, a revelation that jump-started a search for more physical systems where that can happen. A few years ago another graduate student mentioned to me that they had simulated a quasiperiodic system in their ultracold atomic research lab, and I, too, have not stopped chasing the Hofstadter butterfly since. Why would nature care about the difference between rational and irrational numbers so much as to allow for fractional dimensions to be more than a mathematical oddity? Ultracold atomic studies are likely to help physicists answer that question, and I hope to be around to hear about them.

My experience as a researcher has included only a sliver of many topics in modern physics for which ultracold atomic experiments are meaningful. The possibilities are truly numerous. And the quantum simulation revolution is nowhere near over! Researchers continue to push the limits of existing technology to cool gases made up of more elements and execute more manipulations.

Next steps? Quantum chemistry, where molecules form at ultracold temperatures. Ultracold quantum systems that are so large they cannot be called microscopic despite quantum mechanics always being assumed to describe only the smallest of objects. Ultracold systems that can be used to measure fundamental constants in tabletop experiments instead of large accelerators (like CERN's Large

Hadron Collider). Ultracold experiments where a single atom can be poked, prodded, moved around and imaged. And whatever else can give us a window into the fundamentals of our (quantum) world.

About the Author

Karmela Padavic-Callaghan is an assistant professor at Bard High School Early College Manhattan, where she teaches calculus and physics.

Will String Theory Finally Be Put to the Experimental Test?

By Brendan Z. Foster

Many physicists consider string theory our best hope for combining quantum physics and gravity into a unified theory of everything. Yet a contrary opinion is that the concept is practically pseudoscience, because it seems to be nearly impossible to test through experiments. Now some scientists say we may have a way to do exactly that, thanks to a new conjecture that pits string theory against cosmic expansion.

What it comes down to is this question: Does the universe show us all of its quantum secrets, or does it somehow hide those details from our classical eyes? Because if the details can be seen, string theory might not be able to explain them.

One way to rule out the idea is if we can prove that it does not predict an essential feature of the universe. And string theory, it turns out, has a persistent problem describing the most popular account of what went on during the universe's earliest moments after the big bang: inflation.

"Inflation is the most compelling explanation for why our universe looks the way it does and where the structure came from," says Marilena Loverde, a physicist at Stony Brook University. Inflation explains how, in a sense, we got everything in the universe from nothing. The theory says that the early universe went through a phase of extreme expansion. The process magnified random blips in the quantum vacuum and converted them into the galaxies and other stuff around us.

Theorists have had difficulty, though, showing how, or if, inflation works in string theory. The most promising road to doing so–the so-called KKLT construction–does not convince everyone. "It depends who you ask," says Suddhasattwa Brahma, a cosmologist at McGill University. "It has been a lingering doubt in the back of the minds of many in string theory: Does it really work?"

In 2018 a group of string theorists took a series of suggestive results and argued that this difficulty reflected an impossibility—that perhaps inflation just cannot happen in the theory. This so-called de Sitter swampland conjecture claimed that any version of the concept that could describe de Sitter space—a term for the kind of universe in which we expect inflation to take place—would have some kind of technical flaw that put it in a "swampland" of rejected theories.

No one has proved the swampland conjecture, and several string theorists still expect that the final form of the theory will have no problem with inflation. But many believe that although the conjecture might not hold up rigidly, something close to it will. Brahma hopes to refine the swampland conjecture to something that would not bar inflation entirely. "Maybe there can be inflation," he says. "But it has to be a very short period of inflation."

Any limit on inflation would raise the prospect of testing string theory against actual data, but a definite test requires a proof of the conjecture. According to Cumrun Vafa, a physicist at Harvard University and one of the swampland conjecture's authors, researchers can start to build a case for the idea if they can connect it to trusted physical laws. "There are two levels of it," he says. "First is being more confident in the principle. And then there's explaining it."

One approach to building confidence might try to explain what sort of physical rule would limit inflation—or, to put the inquiry in a more practical way: How could string theorists hope to persuade cosmologists to reconsider a favored theory?

These kinds of questions led Vafa and his Harvard collaborator Alek Bedroya to seek out a physics-based reason that could justify the swampland conjecture. They found a candidate in a surprising place. It turns out that inflation already has an unsolved problem looking for a solution: theorists have not all agreed on what happens to the very tiniest quantum details when expansion occurs and magnifies the static of the vacuum.

Physicists lack a working theory that describes the world below the level of the so-called Planck length, an extremely minute distance where they expect the quantum side of gravity to appear. Proponents of inflation have typically had to assume that they can one day work those "trans-Planckian" details into it and that they will not make a big difference to any predictions. But how that step will happen remains an open question.

Vafa and Bedroya have given a simple answer: forget about it. Their new trans-Planckian censorship conjecture asserts that extremely tiny quantum fuzziness should always stay extremely tiny and quantum, despite the magnifying effect of expansion. If this idea is true, it implies limits on the amount of inflation that could happen, because too much of it would mean too much magnification of the trans-Planckian details.

So in a new twist for string theory, researchers can actually look to the sky for some answers. How much inflation is too much for the censorship conjecture? The situation is a bit complicated. Several different models for the actual process of inflation exist, and astrophysicists do not yet have data that confirm any one of them, or the basic idea as a whole, as the correct description of our universe. Researchers have begun working out the limits the new conjecture puts on the many versions of inflation. Some have a built-in way to hide trans-Planckian details, but Loverde says that many of the typical models conflict with the conjecture.

One clear conflict comes from "primordial" gravitational waves. These waves, which theorists expect arise during the inflationary phase, would have left behind a faint but distinct sign in the cosmic microwave background. So far, they have not been seen, but telescopes are actively looking for them. The censorship conjecture would only allow a "ridiculously, unobservably small" amount, Loverde says—so small that any sign of these waves would mean the conjecture does not apply to our universe unless theorists can come up with a different explanation for them.

Does this conjecture really amount to a test of string theory? No, it is too early to say that, according to Vafa. The principles are still just conjectures–for now. "The more one connects these principles together–surprising, unexpected relations–the more it becomes believable why it's true," he says.

About the Author

Brendan Z. Foster is a science writer and audio journalist based in Saint Paul, Minn. He has a Ph.D. in physics from the University of Maryland.

GLOSSARY

dark energy An unknown form of energy that is presumed to explain the accelerating expansion of the universe.

dark matter A proposed undetectable form of matter whose presence explains anomalies in galaxies and certain gravitational effects.

double-slit experiment A classic demonstration in modern physics that light acts as both a wave and a particle, first demonstrated in 1802.

entanglement The state of two particles being connected even at great distances, such that one of them cannot be described without reference to the other.

many-worlds interpretation The attempt to explain the fact that quantum particles can be in multiple locations at the same time.

quantum computing The development of computers which use the concepts of entanglement and superposition to create highly secure encryption methods.

Standard Model The generally agreed upon understanding of subatomic particles in quantum physics.

string theory A theory within quantum physics that attempts to reconcile the Standard Model with gravitational force.

superposition The idea that a quantum particle can be in multiple locations simultaneously, yet when it is observed, only one of those locations can be detected.

uncertainty principle The concept in quantum physics that the position of a particle cannot be identified at the same time as the particle's momentum, and vice versa.

FURTHER INFORMATION

Brown, Brandon, "What Called Them to Physics?," *Scientific American* 1 April 2020, https://blogs.scientificamerican.com/observations/what-called-them-to-physics/

Garisto, Daniel. "'Qutrit' Experiments Are a First in Quantum Teleportation," *Scientific American* 6 August 2019, https://www.scientificamerican.com/article/qutrit-experiments-are-a-first-in-quantum-teleportation/

Gawrylewski, Andrea, "On the Heels of a Light Beam," *Scientific American* 9 December 2021, https://www.scientificamerican.com/article/on-the-heels-of-a-light-beam1/

Horgan, John. "Is There a Thing, or a Relationship *between* Things, at the Bottom of Things?," *Scientific American* 20 September 2021, https://www.scientificamerican.com/article/is-there-a-thing-or-a-relationship-betweenthings-at-the-bottom-of-things/

Michalakis, Spyridon, "How Scientists Solved One of the Greatest Open Questions in Quantum Physics," *Scientific American* 1 August 2020, https://www.scientificamerican.com/article/how-scientists-solved-one-of-the-greatest-open-questions-in-quantum-physics/

Padavic-Callaghan, Karmela, "Quantum Friction Explains Water's Freaky Flow," *Scientific American* 22 February 2022, https://www.scientificamerican.com/article/quantum-friction-explains-waters-freaky-flow/

Sinha, Urbasi, "Quantum Slits Open New Doors," *Scientific American* 1 January 2020, https://www.scientificamerican.com/article/quantum-slits-open-new-doors/

CITATIONS

1.1 100 Years Ago, a Quantum Experiment Explained Why We Don't Fall through Our Chairs by Davide Castelvecchi (February 8, 2022); 1.2 Spooky Quantum Action Passes Test by Ronald Hanson and Krister Shalm (December 1, 2018); 1.3 This Twist on Schrödinger's Cat Paradox Has Major Implications for Quantum Theory by Zeeya Merali (August 17, 2020); 1.4 Quantum Time Twist Offers a Way to Create Schrödinger's Clock by Jonathan O'Callaghan (October 23, 2020); 2.1 Can Quantum Mechanics Save the Cosmic Multiverse? by Yasunori Nomura (June 1, 2017); 2.2 Space: The Final Illusion by Lee Smolin (April 4, 2019); 2.3 What Is Space-time Really Made Of? by Adam Becker (February 1, 2022); 2.4 Can We Gauge Quantum Time of Flight? by Anil Ananthaswamy (October 21, 2021); 2.5 Could Gravity's Quantum Origins Explain Dark Energy? by Conor Purcell (October 28, 2021); 2.6 Escape from a Black Hole by Steven B. Giddings (December 1, 2019); 2.7 The Cosmological Constant Is Physics' Most Embarrassing Problem by Clara Moskowitz (February 1, 2021); 3.1 Basic Quantum Research Will Transform Science and Industry by Irene Qualters and Antoinette Taylor (May 17, 2019); 3.2 Beyond Quantum Supremacy: The Hunt for Useful Quantum Computers by Michael Brooks (October 3, 2019); 3.3 Race for the Quantum Internet by Lee Billings (June 15, 2017); 3.4 'Hybrid' Quantum Networking Demonstrated for First Time by Dhananjay Khadilkar (July 2, 2020); 3.5 Black Holes, Quantum Entanglement and the No-Go Theorem by Zoë Holmes and Andrew Sornborger (July 4, 2021); 4.1 Unexplained Results Intrigue Physicists at World's Largest Particle Collider by Daniel Garisto (March 25, 2021); 4.2 Elementary Particle's Unexpected Heft Stuns Physicists by Daniel Garisto (April 7, 2022); 4.3 In a First, Physicists Glimpse a Quantum Ghost by Karmela Padavic-Callaghan (December 8, 2021); 4.4 New Views of Quantum Jumps Challenge Core Tenets of Physics by Eleni Petrakou (December 29, 2020); 4.5 The Coolest Physics You've Ever Heard Of by Karmela Padavic-Callaghan (January 20, 2020); 4.6 Will String Theory Finally Be Put to the Experimental Test? by Brendan Z. Foster (March 25, 2020).

Each author biography was accurate at the time the article was originally published.

INDEX

A

anthropic principle, 94
artificial general intelligence (AGI), 32–33
Aspect, Alain, 18
atoms, ultracold, 146–147, 149–150

B

Bell, John, 13, 16–18, 20–24, 29–32, 49, 115–116, 120
big bang, 34, 55, 63, 152
black holes, 42–44, 57, 63, 77–88, 102, 123–125
Bohr, Niels, 9–10, 79, 84

C

causal set theory, 62, 94
collapse theories, 28
communications, 22–23, 35, 102, 113–115, 117–118
conformal field theory (CFT), 56–61, 63
consciousness, 26–27, 33
continuous variables (CVs), 119–121
Copenhagen interpretation, 26, 40
cosmic expansion, 73, 96, 152
curvature, 45–46, 78, 94
cybersecurity, 102, 104

D

decoherence, 26–28, 102
dimensional transmutation, 54
discrete variables (DVs), 119–121

E

Einstein, Albert, 5, 10, 14–17, 22, 24, 29, 35–36, 49–54, 56–57, 78, 83, 85, 90–91, 93, 98, 115–116, 120
Event Horizon Telescope (EHT), 77, 84–88
Everett, Hugh, 40–41, 44

F

Feynman, Richard, 106, 123, 145
fluctuation, 52, 83, 86, 107, 128, 130, 132
Frauchiger-Renner paradox, 33

G

Gerlach, Walther, 7–12

gravitational waves, 77, 84–88, 90, 96–97, 154

H

Hawking, Stephen, 42–44, 78–80

hidden variables, 16–22, 115–116

Hubble, Edwin, 91

L

LHCb (Large Hadron Collider beauty), 127–130, 132

light, speed of, 15–17, 20, 29, 35, 43, 49, 80, 84, 97

locality, 18–19, 31–32, 48–53, 80, 82, 84

Los Alamos National Laboratory, -102, 104, 118, 124–125

M

machine learning, 104, 106, 109, 123–125

magnetic field, 8, 10–15

muons, 127–133

N

Newton, Isaac, 48, 66, 68, 98

P

Pauli, Wolfgang, 7, 66, 92

polarization, 18, 21–22, 29–31, 101, 113, 138

Q

quantum bits (qubits), 100, 102–103, 105, 107–110, 112, 120, 123, 143

quintessence, 95–96

R

randomness, 22–23, 143

relativity, 29, 35–36, 49–52, 54–56, 58, 62–63, 73, 78, 82–83, 90–91, 93–94, 97–98, 115

S

Schrödinger, Erwin, 5, 14, 25, 29, 35–36, 50, 67, 70

stars, 12, 35, 73, 80–81, 89, 95–97, 148–150

W

W boson, 131–135

wormholes, 55, 59

Z

Zeilinger, Anton, 18, 21, 116–117